HIS NAME WAS BEN

PAULETTE MAHURIN

ISBN
978-0692264690

Cover by Barbara Gottlieb
www.gottgraphix.com

Published in partnership with
Purple Distinctions Self Publishing
www.purpledistinctions.com
Ventura, CA 93004

Printed in the United States of America

His Name was Ben

Also by Paulette Mahurin

The Persecution of Mildred Dunlap

For My Hubby

Acknowledgments

We sometimes think of an author as a lonely writer banging away on the keyboard, creating characters for readers to love and hate, forming the core of the story. Yet what brings these alive on the page is never a singular task.

Thank you Ryan Cheal, Deb Wall, and Margaret Dodd, my editors. To Christoph Fischer, Lee Fullbright, Dr. William Fox, Deb Norton, Wanda Hartzenberg, Lorna Lee, and Terry Mahurin, a heartfelt debt of gratitude for your feedback, which helped give shape and direction to this narrative.

A special acknowledgment to the real Ben and Sara, who I had the privilege of working with several years ago. They shared their stories and personal feelings with me both together and separately, which was initially written by myself and published as an award-winning short story while I in college. Although this account has been fictionalized (the names of the characters and some scenes have been changed), it is based on actual events. In portraying the integrity of Ben and Sara's relationship, I have taken the liberty to include both of their points of view. The two sides are not of equal content; Sara had more to say. Though some of the facts have been changed, their love story is authentic.

Being deeply loved by someone gives you strength,
while loving someone deeply gives you courage.

Lao-tzu

CHAPTER ONE

It was just past three in the morning when Sara Phillips looked over to the clock on the nightstand. *Tazzie, why can't I sleep like you?* Snuggling close to her Rottweiler, feeling the short black-and-tan hair on her cheek and the robust contour of the dog's chest, she felt a comfort that she was not alone. She wondered how many pills from a nearly full bottle of Ativan in the bathroom would be needed to take her life.

Tazzie, in a deep snoring slumber, twitched a paw into Sara's face as if to say *Stop that kind of thinking.* Sara wasn't that bad off, not yet, but should things continue along as they had, Tazzie's gesture would not deter her; nothing would.

The hours passed, and somewhere in there Sara had drifted off, as her phone woke her just after eight. *Who's calling at this time in the morning?* She jerked up to hear the message on the answering machine.

Listening to her voice, recorded several years ago, full of life and cheer, was opposite to how she felt now. *You've reached Sara. I'd love to talk to you but if I haven't picked up, I'm not home and will get back to you. Please leave a message, and have a great day.* "Sara, it's Dr. Zimmerman…"

She grabbed the phone. "I'm here." Filtering her calls was a necessity, to avoid attrition from the well-wishing callers who further drained her depleted energy.

"We've got good news."

The liveliness in his voice took her breath away. "Really?"

"You've been accepted into a study." The doctor explained some of the specifics to her. "It looks good, Sara. Can you come over to my office now and we'll go over the details and get you started?"

The heart-pounding news sent her trembling, believing that somehow it was a trick, and at the other end of the joke she'd once again be betrayed by the facts. It wasn't Zimmerman she doubted, as he'd always been up-front with her. Rather, it was her experience as a nurse practitioner and what she'd seen that caused the mistrust. She didn't want to drop into fanciful thinking that miracles happen out of nowhere. Not to her, they didn't. But she'd seen things change on a dime with new drugs coming out; she'd seen cures come out of the blue. *What's that about?* Still shaking, replaying the uncharacteristic enthusiasm in Zimmerman's tone, she knew she must take the chance. "Okay," her voice shuddered, "I'll get ready and be there right away."

The shock waves from the conversation decreased as Sara dressed. She thought about the hell she'd been through with Zimmerman guiding her along on the rollercoaster ride her life had become, trying desperately to find something to grab hold of to check the cancer ravaging her body. Since her first oncology appointment with him, once healed from her double mastectomy, she liked him. The look in his eyes, the difficulty he communicated through when there was bad news, and the amount of time he took, allowing her to cry and let her honest feelings out, all told there was integrity and authenticity to this man. Of late she had plunged into a silent darkness that dared to show no light at the end—not until this phone call. *It's a very promising study.* He exuded a certainty, a welcome change from the disappointments.

Sara let Taz outside and grabbed her sunglasses and keys. Fumbling with the car door, she dropped her purse. *Slow down.* The musty dog odor, sunbaked into the car seat, made her squeamish and she opened the windows to air out the stench. An adjustment to the rearview mirror reflected a gaunt face. Punching on the CD player Leonard Cohen's voice sounded, "I'm Your Man," as she stared a few more seconds. "Not enough makeup on my eyes." She smiled at the blush of pink on her cheeks and laughed at the fact she cared about how she looked when it had been so long since she wore even lip gloss. A few deep respirations released the nausea in her belly.

Close to thirty minutes later she pulled into the large medical center parking lot. Noticing Mercedes and BMWs in spots reserved for doctors while Hondas and Fords filled patients slots, *So typical,* she shook her head. Up at the third-floor suite the waiting room was already full of patients. "Dr. Zimmerman told me to just come in."

"Hi Sara, yes," the receptionist smiled, "he's expecting you."

Zimmerman rose from his leather swivel chair. "This is very good news," and pulled out a seat for her. "Come, sit here."

Although she didn't like taking up his time when she knew how busy he was, one look at his relaxed face and the dike burst.

Reaching for a box of tissues, "It's okay to," he handed her one, "let it out."

Zimmerman had been a lifeline for Sara, right up to the last bout of chemo that created more adverse reactions than it benefited. Too many of her questions were addressed with shaking his head and apologizing that he had no answers other than to continue more of the same, which had become intolerable for her.

"Do you genuinely think it'll help me?" This time was different—she didn't fear his response—it felt right in her bones, pained from the cancer spread.

"The results are remarkable. We're seeing full remissions in advanced cases."

On the phone he had mentioned that the side effects were minimal. Still, it seemed too good to be true and she needed reassurance that she wouldn't be putting herself through more bouts of vomiting, diarrhea, and fatigue. "What are the side effects?"

"Mild flu-like symptoms." His deep brown eyes shone with conviction as he said, "And some nausea but it's slight. I'm convinced it's the right thing for you to do."

A snarl of emotions tainted with skepticism pounded her. But the way he spoke and looked at her showed a confidence that put her at ease. Although treatment failures in the past were discouraging, she was never let down because of a false promise from Zimmerman. Desperately wanting to relax into this unexpected turn of events, she knew her decision was made the minute she saw him. "Okay," she dried her eyes and blew her nose. "How long will I be on it before I start to see results?" A sharp pain in her right hip yanked her attention into her body. Wincing, she added, "If they're going to happen."

"Some of the subjects are noticing changes in a couple of weeks with follow-up scans at four, eight, and twelve weeks showing marked reduction in tumor size. There's a lot of favorable data. It's in the final phase before FDA approval. It's perfect timing for you since it's been well tested."

Her airway expanded. "What do I need to do to get started?" He held out a packet of papers. "Fill these out and we'll fax them over to UCLA. They're expecting the paperwork today. Once they okay it, you can start." She looked down at the forms, her slender arm firm.

"Today?"

"Yes," he smiled.

The lights overhead flickered when a handsome man, dressed in ivy-league clothes, opened the door. Noticing a loose screw on the switch plate, he told the receptionist, "Looks like someone needs to tighten that up."

Sara was instantly drawn to him. Curious, she tried to hear what he said, but withdrew into herself when he turned around holding a clipboard and headed toward the empty chair beside her. *Does he see how thin I am?* She concentrated on her wasted appearance. For Sara, the loss of her looks, what she felt was her sensuality, was a loss of self-worth. It surprised her that it even mattered how she looked to him, but it did as his eyes made contact with hers. *He's so good-looking. Am I nuts? I'm a cancer patient and he probably is also.* Aware of him settling into the chair, she tensed. *This is ridiculous.* Shriveling into her skin, the heat of his body made her flush as she fumbled with a magazine, trying to think of something to say to him. "Your first visit?"

He stopped writing, but didn't take his eyes off the form. "Yes."

Seeing his distress, she couldn't help wanting to engage him. "He's a great doctor."

"Um-hum." He carried on writing.

Glancing over at him, she noticed his curly hair and straight nose, how it scrunched up pulling his eyes together when he was thinking. *So cute.* She strained to see his name was Ben. Two seats over, whispers drew her focus away. "I wonder why he's here," said an elderly woman. "He doesn't look ill to me."

Christ, folks, I can hear you! It's true though, he doesn't look ill but he's filling out a patient intake form. Sara's heart sped up as she peeked back and caught sight of his phone number and that he was fifty-two, five years older than she. *I can't believe I'm doing this.* She stood and made her way to the reception desk, "Can I use your restroom?"

Returning to her seat, with his number tucked into her purse, she was glad he didn't look up at her. Feeling awkward because of what she had just done, she watched him reach for a newspaper.

He fussed with the pages, obviously not reading anything.

Sara felt the familiar, agitated energy he exuded and blurted out, "I really like Zimmerman."

"Excuse me?"

"I don't mean to be nosy but I thought… well, it looks like your first visit here and," she took a hard swallow, "I could have used someone to talk to my initial…"

Turning toward her, "I appreciate you making the effort but…" That's when he actually took a look at her and saw how attractive she was, underweight but very pretty with short hair, large hazel eyes, and a small nose surrounded with freckles—an earthy appearance that appealed to him.

With his gaze still on her, "Sometimes it helps to talk to another patient, a stranger," she smiled. "I don't know... I mean, why not?"

Shifting gears, he asked her, "How's it going for you?"

"Today's a good day."

The light in her eyes and lilt as she spoke sat well with him. "That's great."

A nurse opened the door to the back area. "Mr. Gottlieb," she waited, "Ben Gottlieb?"

As he shuffled to get up, Sara said, "Good luck in there."

Looking back at her, his eyes held sorrow. "Thanks. I need it."

There was something about his voice that spread through her body like food, energizing her. *God, he's gorgeous.* She wondered about him, what his story was, and hoped he would be finished before she had to leave.

Sara's initial treatment went smoothly. She was done and on her way home in a couple of hours. The midafternoon sun glared from the bumper of the car in front of hers. Switching lanes to avoid the blinding light, she noticed the orange wildflowers blooming along the highway. She was glad to say goodbye to the unusually cold winter and smiled as she drove past blossoms and leaves filling the empty branches of trees. Approaching her street, she thought of phoning her best friend Ellen to bring her up to speed.

The two women had been friends for the better part of the last twenty-five years, when they met during their senior year in nursing school, and afterwards landed jobs working in the same emergency room. They had been through divorces, tragedies, joys, vacations, and checking off bucket-list items together, but at no time did they ever envision that one of them would have cancer at an early age.

"So, how'd it go?" asked Ellen.

"It went well, better than expected. But..." Doubt resurfaced that maybe she was deluding herself. Sara tried to push it aside, to no avail.

"What?"

"I hope I'm not fooling myself, but the few other patients there did look good."

"You don't need to entertain any skepticism without reason. I doubt that Zimmerman would have built up your hopes on something that wasn't promising. He gave you facts, not a lot of exalted hot air. Right?"

"Yes."

"I can understand your caution. However, this time I think you're safe to hope for the best. With what you've been through, how could it get worse than that?"

"Good point," Sara rested her legs on the coffee table by the couch. "But what if..."

"Let's just see what happens. Today was unanticipated. Breakthroughs and miracles do occur. Hold that thought."

"Yeah," Sara repositioned a pillow behind her back, "you're right. I need to stay positive. How you doing?"

"Tired." Ellen continued, "Some bad stuff came in last night...but you don't need to hear about that. This will perk you up—Kincaid asked Jolie out last night. That guy," she laughed, "can't keep his pants on. Predictable!" Creating levity, Ellen kept Sara up on the emergency room gossip while she was on sick leave.

"I almost forgot. Oh, man, I did something stupid. I can't believe I did it."

"What?"

"There was this guy…" Sara squirmed, "I'm embarrassed to say…"

"What'd you do?"

"This good-looking guy came into Zimmerman's office and sat next to me. Amazing blue eyes, great thin body, the preppie look I like. First visit."

"How'd you know that?"

"I'm getting there. He was filling out an intake form."

"And?"

Sara bumbled, "I glanced over and read what he wrote."

"What's wrong with that? You're human and," Ellen cleared her throat, "hey, if he was that good looking…"

Tazzie hopped up next to Sara, circled, and plopped down. "I noticed his phone number…"

"And?"

"I went to the bathroom and wrote it down. It's in my purse."

"I knew it! He was that good looking!" Ellen was cathartic for Sara, who in the past obsessed over guys and her sex-driven need for them, which had dried up since her diagnosis. "This is the first mention of a man since you took ill. It's a good sign."

"Seriously, El, my first day on the study and I can't stop thinking of this guy. What's wrong with me? And to violate his boundary like that."

"What'd you do that was so wrong? And that you did it, that you're even interested, is terrific!"

"What? You're playing with me, right? You're just playing."

"No, I'm dead serious. You've been out of it for so long. Surgery, chemo, radiation, one cave-in after another, and suddenly your whole life changed. Not only did you get into a study that can save your life, you met a guy. I love it!"

"I wouldn't exactly say," Sara's voice cracked, "I met a guy."

"Did you talk to him?"

"Very little."

"And?"

"He's a patient, for Christ's sake. And I'm getting all excited over him. I barely started a study. I don't even know if it'll work and I'm preoccupied with wanting to be attractive to this guy."

Ellen laughed.

"What's so damn funny?"

"It's healthy." Ellen continued laughing.

Sara listened to the bubbling relief pouring out of Ellen, the lightness in her voice, and realized how ridiculous she was being. After what she'd been through, it was absurd that she felt her moral compass was out of whack because of a stranger she sat next to that she'd probably never see again.

You going to phone him?"

"No! Are you kidding?"

"What are you going to do with his number?"

"Throw it out," she rubbed Tazzie's head, "as soon as we get off the phone."

"Let me know after you call him," Ellen laughed. "I gotta go and get ready for work."

"Okay, hope it's better than last night."

Feeling hot and sticky from the warm day, Sara showered. Drying herself before a mirror, she examined the scars from the mastectomies that couldn't be repaired cosmetically while the cancer cells still raged through her body and glowed in scans. For the first time since the horror began, she wondered if she would have that plastic surgery reparation. *Ellen's right. It's pleasing to think of being with a man.*

CHAPTER TWO

Sara rummaged through her refrigerator to find something to eat before going to bed. She decided on a baked potato she'd picked at the night before. While adding a dollop of sour cream and popping the plate into the microwave, her dog sat staring. "How about lending me some of your appetite, Taz?" Tazzie raised a paw and barked. "You're not going to let up till you get your treat." Sara reached into the stash of dog cookies and threw one. "Good catch." She grabbed her supper and they went to the bedroom.

An hour later, with her food barely touched, Sara sat in bed trying to finish the last chapter of the book she was reading. The sweltering spring weather, similar to a particular March evening two years ago when her symptoms first started, triggered memories.

She remembered waking around two in the morning, her nightgown drenched in perspiration. *Why am I so hot?* Sleeping, Taz showed no signs of panting from a heated night. It took a hefty dose of Benadryl to get Sara back to sleep.

A week passed and there was another episode of pre-dawn sweats, but this time her dog's frantic sniffing and nudging at her right breast woke her. "Tazzie, stop!" The mammogram her doctor ordered had shown a suspicious calcification.

The day Ellen drove her to the breast surgeon, the bright bougainvillea along the roadside strangling other plants reminded her that aberrant cancer cells in her own body might be taking over. All around, the signs of spring with bees and birds busily pollinating made her think of women with new life growing in their wombs. It filled her with a deep sorrow that she might be facing her own mortality. Negative thinking relentlessly flooded her mind, like a hose that had sprung a leak. *There's a mass* kept replaying.

How many times do I have to relive this? Blinking away tears, she moved her hand under the sheet into her nightie, to the rough wrinkles and edges of scar tissue that had failed to heal in normal time because of infection, delaying chemo and radiation treatment. Touching the place where her breasts were removed, parts of her body that had given pleasure, now felt only the pressure of her fingers.

Remembering the night before the surgery, crying to Ellen that the sleep medication wasn't working, she tried to ease her fear; what she didn't want to face was that she'd no longer be attractive or desirable to a man. *Did Ben trigger this? I was feeling so good. Why does this keep coming back up?*

Wanting to escape the mental pictures that refused to leave, she gazed at the page before her, trying to forget the trauma. Unable to stop the avalanche of thinking, she got up and put a load of laundry into the washing machine. The low rotating vibration against Sara's body stirred sensations and she was once again reminded of Ben. As the wash swished in the sudsy water, she thought of how his eyes made her feel, the motion of his hand—slow and suggestive—gliding the pen over the form he filled out. She imagined his fingers on her body, moving gently between her legs with his lips on her neck. The meager tingles of arousal were a revival she welcomed.

Sara relished the idea of being with a man anew, but first things first; it was way too soon to know what would happen with the study. *I'm so out of shape. I hope I get my strength back so I can exercise.*

Prior to becoming ill, she was compulsive about walking miles with her dog, and when she could no longer do that, she took to her stationary bike. Of late, she was too lethargic to do much more than walk from room to room. She missed being outdoors among the hikers and bikers, people on horseback, and tourists coming to relax in beautiful Ojai, where she lived. *Please give me energy,* she spoke to the mysterious ethers. *It's all I ask. For now,* she laughed.

CHAPTER THREE

Sara found out about Ojai, the small California town nestled among oak, pepper and eucalyptus trees, while working in the emergency room. Having just come off a stint of twelve-hour shifts, she wanted to veg out. Knowing there would be way too many distractions at home to relax, she researched spas within driving distance and found one located in Ojai. It was seventy miles from where she lived and a twenty-minute drive to Ellen, who commuted into Los Angeles County where they both worked. After spending a week immersed in its lush natural beauty, on a fluke she met a realtor who offered to show her around.

She never regretted the spontaneous decision to move there ten years earlier when she purchased a 1950s ranch house and fixed it up. Painting the walls multicolors brought it alive, with art, pottery, and photos of family and friends making it a cozy nest. Large windows framed the abundant foliage, like living in a tree house. It was what she needed to put a divorce behind her and start a new life with renewed purpose.

The cancer diagnosis changed that, until the unexpected occurred—being accepted into the study and the buzz over meeting Ben. With attention riveted on his phone number, the rational cells in Sara's brain ping-ponged back and forth. *What would I say if I called him?* Her mouth went dry, reminding her of telling her parents about the results from the biopsy.

Recollecting the two agitated days and sleepless nights staring hesitatingly at the telephone, detesting every aspect of the chaotic situation violently forced on her, she cringed. Knowing that her mother Rosalie was stoic with a rough-edge attitude and would handle it didn't allay the gut-twisting nervousness that the news could endanger her father Irving's health. He'd already had two heart attacks.

There was also her brother Jack, who she hoped wasn't home to complicate things. She remembered being told by an aunt that ever since Sara was a baby, "Something was wrong with him." When her brother first left home, she was so young she didn't recall much about him. She knew from an early age that when he was around, the house grew silent and uncomfortable. Years later, she learned he was schizophrenic. The extra stress of Jack being there wasn't needed.

When Sara finally got the courage to dial, Rosalie picked up. "Hello."

Sara's abdomen anxiously gurgled. "Hi mom. How's dad?"

A blunt laconic, "Today's okay," was nothing new. Neither was the long uninvolved pause, waiting for Sara to speak.

Trying to find a way to say it, "Mom…" Apprehensive to utter the words, fearful that she would then have to face them, Sara flushed hot as though she was running a fever. With disbelief pulsing through her veins, she quietly hoped she'd hear compassion, that everything would be okay, that maybe there had been a mistake. Anything encouraging that would lessen the shocking news she was about to tell her mother.

Rosalie grunted out a curt "What do you want?"

Her mother's coldness lit Sara's stomach on fire. Taking in a deep slow breath, "I have bad news…"

Rosalie came back with a razor-sharp "What?" When no instant response came from her daughter, she smacked her lips. "Oh for Christ's sake, Sara, what's the bad news now?"

Why do you have to be so damn difficult? Give me a break! She wanted to throw the phone down. "I don't know how to say this."

The line went silent.

Walking through the narrowest of doors her mother barely left open, she blurted out, "I have breast cancer." Sick inside, she told her mother that the diagnosis was the worst kind of malignancy and it was in her nodes. What started in the right breast showed radiographic spread to the left, necessitating a double mastectomy, the sooner the better.

Rosalie gasped.

Feeling as if she'd diffused out of her body and was watching strangers discuss a horror film, Sara gripped the edge of a table to ground herself. Back to the unthinkable reality she was slogging through as if pulled under by wet sand, her legs became heavy. Sinking lower and lower, she asked, "Where's daddy?"

Rosalie blasted, "Irving, come here!"

Hearing the babbling between them as Rosalie told him the news, Sara felt like her head was going to explode. The room went in and out of focus with her father's wheezing, echoing distress. "Dad, please don't get worked up over this."

"I'm fine, Sara..." Irving's voice cracked. "And you will be too. You've got the best insurance and doctors—that's what's important. I have great faith in our medical system. It's kept me alive, hasn't it?"

Sara understood he talked to ease his pain. So did she, when she switched the topic from the diagnosis to the only thing that came to mind. "Any word from Jack?" She rubbed her temples in a circular motion to release her tension.

"No, not for six months now. His medication must be working." He went on about current psych drugs and how they seem to be getting results.

"That's good to hear. Dad, I need to get going now."

Images of that exhausting brain-fogging conversation faded as Sara's attention went back to Ben. Thinking about him lifted her spirits, compared with the jarring drain from her mother's heart-piercing words. She wondered what his story was. Although he looked worried that day at Zimmerman's, he didn't look physically ill. *It couldn't be that bad. I wonder if he's on a study.*

Wanting to review the data from hers, she went to the computer to read up on it. Within seconds the information was before her. *This looks too good to be... Oh man, they're talking of a cure.* Just then the phone rang.

"Hey. Perfect timing."

"You sound perky," said Ellen.

"I was just reading some of the other info Zimmerman told me to check into about the study. Lots of great results."

"I know," chirped Ellen, "I asked around."

"And?"

"You really did get lucky."

"Oh El, bless you! Exactly what I needed to hear. And from you."

"Yeah, the truthsayer speaks," Ellen laughed.

"That's funny. Reminds me of 'The Emperor's New Clothes.'"

"Speaking of no clothes, did you phone?"

"No!"

"Whoa, what's with the backlash?"

"I'm sorry. It's stupid to have so much attention on him, but I can't help myself."

"I know. I know. Please, listen to me. I'm just playing around to lighten things up. I'm not judging. I want you to be happy, Sara."

"I know you do, El. It's just that…"

Ellen, hearing Sara's long sigh said, "I know sex is a big deal for you. And why. I know how important it is for you to feel attractive and wanted. There's nothing wrong with that. Absolutely nothing."

"Thanks for understanding."

"You know it's totally okay to phone. It's okay to fantasize over him. That's a good thing. Focus on anything that helps your mood."

"I really appreciate your saying that. I do wonder what his situation is."

CHAPTER FOUR

Prior to his making the decision to go down to Southern California, Ben had a full battery of tests at Stanford, including scans and a biopsy. Normally calm, he lost his cool when he went before the Tumor Board. He was told that he had a 25 percent, one-year survival rate. Pushing back his cuticles to pacify his nerves, *How the hell did I miss this?* He tried to remember if there were symptoms that he'd overlooked, but there were none. By the time the first sign of indigestion appeared, his condition was too far-gone.

"It wasn't your fault, Ben," came from one of the doctors on the board. "That's the problem with this type of cancer. When anything becomes apparent, it's usually advanced."

Ben took a hard swallow, "And you're sure about it being pancreatic cancer?" He had hoped that it was a mistake. Even a less-aggressive cancer, like Lance Armstrong's advanced testicular cancer that had a strong cure rate, would be better news than this.

"We sent the slides out to Yale for confirmation. It's the best lab in the country."

Another doctor interrupted. "Of course, with advances in research, there could be a breakthrough any time now."

Ben slumped in a heated sweat. "Oh, my God."

The oncologist sitting next to Ben put a hand on his shoulder. "There is some chemotherapy."

"And what would that do? It's just palliative. That's what you told me, right?"

"That's correct, Ben."

"With the side effects." He looked around at the group in lab coats for some sign, something else that could offer him hope. "What kind of choice is that?"

The female doctor responded empathetically, "Not an easy one, Ben."

The room went silent for what seemed like forever until Ben spoke from a daze. "I need to be with this for now."

There he was with Stanford's finest, gathered to offer him his best fighting chance, and in his case there didn't seem to be one.

After that gruesome meeting, Ben wanted to talk to his brother Michael, a surgeon, to see if there were other options that may have been overlooked. He arranged to meet him at the Palo Alto Creamery Fountain & Grill downtown.

Ben sat at the packed restaurant, watching Silicon Valley's young twenty-to-thirty set, glued to their iPads and smart phones, when his phone buzzed. "What's up, Mike? Where are you?"

"I just got out of surgery. I'll clean up and be there in about fifteen minutes." In the background blared the overhead speaker, summoning doctors to stations and nurses to pick up phones—the usual cacophony at Stanford Medical Center. "Go ahead and order. Get me a hot pastrami on toasted rye with coleslaw."

Ben regretted that his days of eating that way were over. The diagnosis prompted him to consult a dietician as part of an attempt to regain his health. Aware that Steve Jobs extended his life with an alternate health program, including a vegetarian diet, motivated Ben to give it a try. Not to that extent, but he did agree to cut back on simple whites—white sugar, rice, and pasta—and avoid fried, high-fat food. When the nutritionist said, "You are what you eat, so eat healthy," he knew that although it wasn't a cure-all, it did make sense.

A woman carrying a tray with plates of food walked past and set them down on the table next to him. The aroma of grilled beef sent his stomach into spasms, pouring acid into his throat. He motioned the waitress over to his table, gave Michael's order and his own. "I'll have the veggie sandwich." When she walked away he popped a couple of antacid tablets into his mouth.

Their meals arrived at the table just before Michael did. "Sorry about that." He pulled the chair in, grabbed hold of his sandwich, and took a bite. "So how'd it go?"

"Not good."

Michael took a spoonful of coleslaw and swallowed it down with a sip of water. "What did Bentley have to say?" referring to an oncological surgeon Michael knew on the board.

"That the prognosis is poor." He paused to avoid sinking into how hopeless it all was. "You didn't look at my chart?"

"It's too close for me, Ben. But if you want me to…"

"No, no, you're right. I don't want to do that to you."

Michael put down his sandwich and looked at Ben. "It's not my area," his voice was unsteady. "You don't want to do the conventional chemo?"

"For what? A few added months along with those side effects. I don't know what to do. I can't believe there's nothing else."

"Well, there may be something," Michael was hesitant. "I do know of someone doing advanced work using drugs that were prescribed for other cancers not yet approved for pancreatic that show promise. It's not a sure thing but I trust the person involved. If I were you, I'd give it a shot."

Ben looked up expectantly.

"Remember the other Michael, my roommate from medical school?"

"Zimmerman?"

"Yes, he's an oncologist doing studies at UCLA."

"You have my attention." Ben was not convinced. He wanted to grab onto something but needed data, not just words or attempts to make him feel better. His brother was a realist, a hard, cold-facts doctor, a surgeon, but he also knew that up till now Michael had not faced any close personal loss in his life. "Do you honestly think he can help me?"

"Yes," Michael smiled. "And he'll see you." He explained to Ben that Zimmerman was doing his own tests, stretching the policy on safe moral research practices, but he was dealing with last-resort, no-other-hope patients, some of whom were very high profile with political connections. "Zimmerman is noted for testing FDA-approved cancer drugs on other cancers they weren't sanctioned for. The guy has balls. He's seeing results, Ben."

"Seriously?" Synapses firing chemistry of hope crept back into Ben's system. "That's encouraging. Thanks, Mike."

After that conversation, Ben decided to take a leave of absence from his job in the legal department at NASA to see Michael Zimmerman for a consultation.

Westwood, bordered by Bel Air and Beverly Hills, is the home of UCLA. Ben sat in his hotel room in Westwood

Village, reflecting back on the lunch with his brother several weeks ago. The village was a suitable location because of its close proximity to UCLA's medical school and hospital. He also wanted to stay in this upbeat place, filled with boutiques, restaurants, and theaters, to distract his mind from the recent doom and gloom. It was close to Zimmerman when he did rounds at UCLA, and only a forty-five-minute drive to his office in a densely populated agricultural city. Ben felt more at home around a college campus that reminded him of Palo Alto.

Relieved that his abdominal pain had lessened since Zimmerman started him on a trial drug, he began relaxing and got out to explore and enjoy the sights. After a walk in town, the red light on the phone was blinking. The message from his brother said, "How's it going? I'm done for the day so give me a call."

"Mike, you're off early." Ben, eyeing the mirror as he spoke, thought his skin looked lighter from when he was in Palo Alto.

"How are you?"

"I think I'm doing better. Zimmerman has me on some drug. I've got less nausea."

"You still have any?"

"Yeah, but it depends on what I eat," he grinned. "I've been fudging it a bit."

"That'll do it." Michael was distracted by the voice of a woman in the background. "Hold on a minute... Candace, I'm on the phone with Ben."

"You're both home?" referring to the fact that Michael and his wife usually worked late most weeknights.

"Yeah, we're going to a dinner tonight. She's getting an award for her work with the Pediatric Center."

"You're a good team." Watching his reflection in the mirror turn serious, Ben asked, "Any word from the folks?"

"The usual. Have you talked to them?"

"Who's to talk to? I haven't been in touch with them for months."

"You haven't told them?" asked Michael.

"No, and I don't plan to."

CHAPTER FIVE

In the days that followed, with several treatments under her belt, Sara's stamina began to increase, which enabled her to get out for short walks with Taz. Regaining strength prompted her to do catch-up housework and handle a few odds and ends that had fallen into disrepair. Becoming more motivated, she embarked on the first good spring-cleaning she'd done in two years. While dusting her bookshelves, she thumbed through a photo album, appreciating how she appeared in better times. She smiled at a snapshot of herself, a slim, well-framed, woman with radiant chameleon hazel eyes, long curly, reddish-brown hair tied back in a twisty, and a speckling of freckles around her cheeks. *I hated those freckles while growing up,* she laughed, *until they became fashionable on models in magazines.*

Coming across a picture taken a few months before the surgery, she looked at her fully formed beautiful breasts with just enough cleavage showing, a sad reminder of the torment she went through as she prepared for a double mastectomy. Then the sorrow was endless, wave upon unrelenting wave crashing in on her. With each surge of tears came the memories: her first bra, the first time a boy unlatched it and touched her breasts, hands roaming sensually on nipple stimulation bringing her close to orgasm, and how good her breasts looked in a bathing suit or a low-cut dress.

The restless night before the operation, standing in front of her mirror sobbing, she caressed her bosom, watching her nipples expand and contract, fondling the curves, the smoothness, and feeling for the mass that she wanted to rip off her chest. "Go away!" At close to three in the morning, when crying failed to exhaust her, she phoned Ellen, "I can't sleep."

"Do you want me to come over?"

"Why did this happen?"

"Sara, is there anything I can do for you?" Ellen's heartbreak bled from every word.

"I can't stop thinking." Floods of agony poured over an inconsolable Sara. "I feel like I'm going insane."

"Did you take what they gave you for sleep?"

"It didn't work," she pounded a fist on her pillow.

"Take another one."

"I already did."

"Make yourself a warm bath and get in. I'm coming over."

Two weeks into the chemotherapy, when the trauma from the surgery started to calm, another emotional crisis flared when Sara started to lose handfuls of her hair. "I've lost my femininity," she cried to Ellen. "Am I still a woman?"

"Sara, it's the loss talking. It'll pass, just hang in there."

"Easy for you to say when it's not happening to you!" she protested. "I hate my ugly body!"

"How you're feeling is not how you look. Your body is beautiful. Your hair will grow back."

Fury turning to tears, "My breasts won't," Sara broke down. Four weeks after completing the first round of chemo, her hair started to return. "Things are looking better," she told Ellen.

Sara stared at the photo of herself at a perfect weight before she became ill, remembering how self-conscious she felt when Ben first looked at her. *What'd he think of my scrawny figure?* Wearing clothes to cover up her bony limbs, she worried, *When am I going to get my appetite back so I can put some meat on?*

Later that afternoon at her computer she typed in the name Ben Gottlieb, with nothing of any value coming to the screen. Images of his strong facial features surfaced, those astonishing blue eyes, and she pondered if there was more to him than his good looks. From the gentleness in his voice she surmised he was a kind man. Her reverie was curtailed when Tazzie nuzzled that she wanted a walk.

As appointments continued at UCLA, Sara spoke with other patients who raved about their positive results. She, too, was experiencing encouraging changes. Sleeping through the night was more commonplace. *Probably*, she thought, *because I have the strength to take longer walks.* Each day as her fortitude increased so did her morale and fantasizing about Ben. Nightmares intermingled with new visions of pleasure. On one particular night she dreamed of floating on a wave, moving up and down riding the curl to shore where a lifeguard in the buff was on duty, his muscles glistening in the sun. Just as he offered to oil her down, she awoke with her hand on her crotch inside her pajama bottoms masturbating. Reaching to the nightstand, she got her vibrator out of the drawer. Thoughts of absent breasts, no nipples left to stimulate, ran through her mind. *Don't go there. I don't need to dwell.* Kicking off her pajama bottoms, she spread her legs and continued to work the rhythmic motion over her clitoris until spasms rose up her spine and exploded into tiny energy particles scattering over her body. Off came the internal physical and emotional suppression from months of anguish with chemo and radiation. *I love sex!*

She recalled her first sexual encounter, experimenting in high school at sixteen. Her first orgasm didn't happen until she was nineteen, in college, when her sensuality awakened. The ultimate turn-on was marrying Henry. The sparks never had a chance to die by the time he dumped her, three years into their marriage, for a metaphysical cult he was involved in. After that, she shied away from sentimental investments with men. Now, speculating about Ben was opening her up to what she hoped might turn into something promising.

Appreciating the last of the tingling sensation yet in her body, she instinctively knew, *My sex drive is returning—I bet the treatment is working.*

CHAPTER SIX

Sara was right. And the treatments continued to progress at an intense pace with minimal side effects—mild flu-like symptoms, slight fever and muscle aches—that were less severe the longer she was on them. In only a few weeks, the night sweats diminished and her appetite was returning. As she became stronger, she persisted in her mission to find information about Ben.

"Did you check into his area code?" asked Ellen.

"I hadn't thought of that."

"You might get some results."

It turned out to be useful advice. The phone number and name led her to a Ben Gottlieb who lived in Palo Alto, an attorney who worked at NASA. *Why would he be seeing Zimmerman when there's Stanford and UCSF up there?* It didn't make sense. "He lives in Palo Alto," she told Ellen.

"You found that in the search?"

"Yeah, but what's he doing down here?"

"Good question. You going to call him?"

When it came right down to it Sara was afraid to be with a man, fearful that she'd look disfigured to him. This fear ran deep in her to a confused jumble that lived in the murky recesses of her psyche, in subconscious lifelong incidents that started bubbling up in nightmares shortly after her mastectomies. What she had successfully kept blocked for so many years was creeping back in, one dream, one image, and one memory at a time—the pieces of a puzzle that had not yet formed a whole picture. But, entertaining the idea of receiving affirmation from Ben that she was attractive was a salve. And wanting to feel normal, she continued to obsess over him. Programming Ben's number into her cellphone, she imagined him at the other end, smiling when he saw it ringing. *This is nuts!* Vacillating between old flirty patterns and her hesitation, she played with her phone, opening it to his name and closing it. *I'm getting nowhere fast.*

"Well?" Ellen repeated, "You going to phone him?"

Squirming in her seat, a meek "No" escaped as Sara's heart pounded in her head.

"You're gonna drive yourself nuts if you don't make the call," Ellen laughed.

"It's not funny," whined Sara.

"I know. I'm not laughing at you. It just came out."

Sara, a bundle of tension, remained quiet.

"Tell me, what do you think is going to happen if you do it?" asked Ellen.

"I don't want to lie about why I'm phoning, and I feel silly telling him."

"Just phone and be honest about it. Say you'd like to meet him. Maybe it would help both of you?"

"Hmm…" Sara groaned.

"You don't have to do it, if you don't want to."

Clicking a nail on her tooth, "I'm stuck," Sara looked out her bedroom window at a squirrel on an overhead wire, running back and forth.

"Talk to me."

"Maybe it's too soon for me to be contemplating meeting someone. It's so stupid…he's a cancer patient."

"So are you, Sara. You're also a woman. And if the cancer taught you anything, it's to live while you can. No guarantees for tomorrow."

Sara shot back, "Oh, that's helpful."

"I'm not being disparaging. Listen to me. We've both seen it in the ER. We collectively walk around deluded that the future is a guarantee when we know it's not true."

"Yeah."

"I understand your predicament. I sense your pain. I sure as hell don't want you doing something that'll compromise your treatments, but I also know you. I know what a relationship with a man could mean for you. We both do."

"Relationship? Who's talking about that? I just want to meet him. What kind of future could there be between us?"

"What do you think is going on? You can't stop thinking about him and I hear the animation in your voice."

"El, I don't know what to do." Sara switched the receiver to nestle it between her left cheek and shoulder. She rubbed the sore spot on her right ear.

"Follow your heart. Let it do the walking. And for God's sake Sara, don't lose sight of the gift you've received getting on the study. It's a miracle. Try entertaining some gratitude and keep your perspective on where you were a few weeks back."

As shadows of the sun drifted behind the mountains, Sara knew they'd been on the phone for over an hour and that Ellen would continue as long as she needed her. "Ellen!"

"Yes?"

"I love you!"

"It's mutual."

Fumbling with the phone, she looked at Tazzie and remembered when she first saw her at the shelter whimpering to be free. Sara's life had been empty until she got a dog. Having a pet gave her the companionship she lacked with friends at school. It also taught her that there were other ways to be, not filled with pretense, being polite to win favor, or telling others what they wanted to hear to gain acceptance, which never helped build friendships anyway. Sara got down on the floor next to Tazzie. "I don't think I can do it."

Taz, forehead wrinkled and head titled to one side, looked like she wondered what the trouble was. She relaxed back down and rolled over to show her underside, as if to say, *Be open. I'm here. We'll get through this together.*

"Thank you, girl."

The next morning Sara woke to her dog's licking, *Feed me.* Sara grabbed hold of her, rubbed a hand over the dog's saddle region sending her leg moving—the harder she scratched, the faster it went. "Got your sweet spot, girl?" Her hand on Taz's chest moved up and down to the motion of the dog's breathing, bringing home the mystery and marvel of living things. *It's astonishing how any of this happens. My heart beats twenty-four-seven along with my lungs working tirelessly. This moment is all there is. Perspective, I mustn't lose it, despite my insecurities.*

Sara got up, fed Taz, and made herself a cup of coffee. By a stroke of luck, her phone rang and it was Zimmerman who called to let her know her last set of lab results were starting to show improvements. "What does this mean?" she asked.

"The drug is taking hold," he replied, and went on to say it was what they wanted to see. "Follow-up tests will be done but we're on the road now."

"Wow, thanks! You just made my day!" *I've been blessed with a second chance.* She reflected back on the last two years and remembered what Ellen said to her about gratitude. *Ellen's right.*

Inhaling the fumes of caffeine brought back the last treatment she's had, sitting around with other patients and a nurse who was raving about the successes. "It's a miracle drug. I've never seen anything like it throughout my years of practice." Sara thought the nurse just wanted to make her feel good, until she met one of the women from an earlier trial. "I had metastases to my brain and bones. They're 90 percent resolved." The words were not important compared to the glow on the woman's face, a walking miracle of cheer and goodwill energizing everyone around her. There were others, even one more dramatic—a complete cure. At first Sara choked on these stories but slowly accepted they were real, as if she was seeing the Resurrection with her very own eyes.

Distracted by Taz's food dish banging around indicating it was empty signaled Sara it was time to take her for a walk. With fresh air, the encouragement from Zimmerman, and contemplation clearing her head, she decided to contact Ben. Worst-case scenario, he wouldn't be interested and she runs into him at Zimmerman's. *So what?* She felt more confident. *If I don't do anything, then nothing happens.* When ten o'clock rolled around, she dialed.

Ben was toweling off from his shower when he heard his cell phone ring. Opening it to a strange number and no message, he wondered if it might be someone connected with Zimmerman. He hit return and when a woman answered said, "This is Ben Gottlieb. Did you just try to reach me?" He tightened the grip on his towel and went to sit on his bed while he listened to a strange new voice fumbling to say something intelligent, and then he remembered. "You're the one sitting next to me my first day at Zimmerman's?"

Sara shifted about feeling foolish that she'd attempted such a dumb move. Thoughts of anything worthwhile vanished, confidence gone, as she withered with embarrassment, and "Yes" was all she thought to say.

Clearly taken aback, he asked, "Did they give you my number?"

"No, absolutely not." She tried to think of some lie, something less humiliating than she spied on him because he was cute and she was being nosy, but her mind went blank.

"Hello."

"Yes, I'm still here. Please hear me out for a minute."

Ben waited.

"I noticed when you filled out your form."

"Um-hum."

"And, well," she coughed, "excuse me."

Squeezing his grip on the phone, "Can you get to the point? I need to get going."

"I saw your number and memorized it," shot out.

"You did what?"

The edge in his speech sent a hot flush through her belly. "Please let me explain why."

"I don't have time for this. You've got a lot of nerve. That is personal information."

"I know. I'm sorry."

"I have to go. I trust you'll delete my number and leave me alone."

"Wait! We both have cancer. What's the harm? Please don't hang up."

Again he went silent, waiting.

"What do you have to lose by just listening to me?" Not hearing him hang up, she continued, "Zimmerman is my doctor. I would have assumed you had cancer even if I hadn't seen the form. All his patients...he's an oncologist. And I know most are palliative. That's his specialty."

"Why are you phoning me?"

"You caught my attention, we had a few nice words, and I figured out why not get in touch with you." Courageously, she told him she'd just been approved to be on a clinical trial, the only positive news she'd had in over two years, the same day he came for his first visit, and clarified why she had waited this long, several weeks, to phone him. "I wanted to start my study first," she explained. "I was afraid that it might not work and I'd be in no shape to connect with a new friend. It's been going well."

Intrigued with the success she was having with the treatments, it hadn't dawned on him that she was attracted to him. "So then, why now?"

"I've had you on my mind. I'd like to meet you."

Oddly amused and now understanding her flirtation, the sensual softening of her voice, he smiled. "I'm presently not in a good place to meet women. I hope you'll understand that I'm..."

"Ben," taking the liberty to call him by his first name, "I've lived through it. Perhaps I can offer you something no one else can?" Nervously doodling squiggles on a notepad, "And now being on the study myself... Plus, I'm also an NP."

"NP?"

"Nurse practitioner. Sorry."

That changed the equation. "Oh," he responded.

Hearing the shift in his tone helped her feel more composed, and after a few minutes she convinced him it might not be a bad idea for them to get together. He would be in Oxnard the following Wednesday for an office visit with Zimmerman, and they could meet somewhere in Ventura County for a cup of coffee.

Enthusiastically, she chose the place and gave him directions.

"See you then," he hung up.

"I did it!" she crowed to her dog. "I can't believe I'm going to see him!"

One minute Ben's mind was set in a fixed direction, to concentrate on his treatment and only that. The next instant a switch gets flipped in his brain and it's a green light to meet a woman. In hindsight, he was surprised that he veered from his path and wondered where the detour would take him. Although curious about the success she was having, he knew he could read up on studies, consult with others directly involved—still nothing sparked him in that direction. Reflecting back on what she said about being an NP and perhaps being able to offer help, *I don't want to talk about my health.* His muscles tightened at the thought of opening up, not just to a woman who happened to be a nurse, but to anyone. Why he shifted gears when she mentioned that, he didn't understand. *Maybe it's an excuse to see her? There is something about her,* echoed in his head. *But what?* Knowing better than to be drawn in by an attractive woman, and he did notice how pretty she was, he realized that he needed human contact other than the medical team taking care of him or a support group that hadn't resonated. It was normal to want to break out of the unnatural environment he'd been involved in with white coats, medicinal odors, professional consulting, and connect with something ordinary, familiar to him. *Why her?* Replaying the sensual innuendo she tried to cover up in her voice, he laughed that he was slow on the uptake. *Why wouldn't a cancer patient want the same things a healthy person does?* He liked entertaining that notion. *I hope I'm not making a mistake, but what do I have to lose?*

CHAPTER SEVEN

Sara settled into a moderately exuberated comfort, looking forward to her date with Ben. It didn't hurt that they had Zimmerman in common, which gave them something to talk about. *I can't believe the changes I've had since he put me on the study.* She looked out the bay window in her kitchen, through the sycamore tree, up to the sky where a few cumulus clouds slowly moved by, and wondered how Ben's treatment was going.

Rethinking what she could talk about with Ben, *How much should I share with him? I don't want to tell him I've had my breasts removed. But how do we avoid the obvious unspoken truth of our situations?* Needing something to hold on to, bringing up Zimmerman seemed the best idea. She thought back to the first few visits when he'd started supervising her chemotherapy and helped calm her frighteningly uncontrollable thinking. She recalled the day his meditative powers diminished when he told her, "You're at the limit of the radiation you can receive." The creases under his eyes accentuated as he spoke. "The scan still shows hot areas. We can try another round of chemo."

"No! I don't want to go through more vomiting, diarrhea, fatigue." Then, like breathing through molasses, she coughed out, "With such a poor prognosis."

Continuing to reflect back, she thought of the visit with Zimmerman when he recounted the harsh facts about what she could bargain on. *The life expectancy is twenty-five months.* He was right about the numbers. Nine months after the diagnosis, surgery, and treatments, she felt enlarged nodes in the center of her rib cage. *This can't be.* When she felt pain in her pelvic area, a bone scan confirmed the metastases. Angst increasing, she upped her intake of anti-anxiety and sleeping pills until she existed in a fog of slurred speech and poor quality of life.

Nope, not going to bring this up with Ben. It's too much of a downer. If anything, I'm going to keep it light. I don't want to turn him off. But what if he asks? Remembering the days of dread, *Thank God that's behind me now and my body is responding favorably. I'll just focus on what's happening now and how well it's going. Concentrate on what will help give Ben confidence.*

Shifting her attention back to her date with Ben, her focus went to what she'd wear. *Everything I own is baggy on me.* She went to the Eddie Bauer outlet store in Camarillo and picked a pair of jeans and a jean shirt; size four fit perfectly and didn't make her look too thin.

Tutti's was Sara's favorite restaurant in Ventura, just past the Buenaventura Mission in the heart of the gentrified downtown area. She loved the restaurant's courtyard with stone features and original brick. *It's so quaint and romantic.* Her appetite was improving and she was looking forward to ordering her favorite pizza. That and Ben consumed her thoughts while she got ready.

Driving down Highway 33, singing along with Michael Buble's "Feeling Good," she glanced in the rearview mirror to check how she looked, when she noticed her lipstick was smeared onto her teeth. Trying to rub it off, she missed seeing a dog on the curb about to run into the street. "Oh no!" Swerving to avoid it, she ran into a pole, bending the front of her car and releasing the air bag. The searing pain in her chest was instant. "Noooooo!"

Sara, hearing the sirens and a man cautioning about smoke coming out of the hood of her car, panicked. Her attempts to break loose were futile. Resistance from the inflated nylon pouch spewing a powdery odor was too great for her to prevail against. "Help! I can't move!"

The crowd backed away as paramedics rushed to the car. "Easy, easy there, you'll be okay," said the tall male rescue worker.

Burning rib pain pressed in on her. Chemicals stung her eyes. "I can't breathe!" she gasped.

They worked fast and gingerly to get her out onto a stretcher as the fire truck arrived.

"Ouch!" Trying to get air into her constricted chest while the other paramedic, a female, listened with a stethoscope, Sara moaned, "Oh please, not a punctured lung."

"Shh," the woman smiled at her, "let me finish." The cold instrument moved over Sara's flesh as the ambulance headed toward the hospital. "Your lungs sound clear."

Ben paced the courtyard of Tutti's paying attention to newcomers with what he remembered of Sara's description. *Where is she?*

When asked by the maître d' if he'd like to be seated, he replied, "No, I'll wait till my date gets here." After forty-five minutes the man approached him again to see if he might like a glass of water. "No, thank you," his gut churned. "It doesn't look like I'll be staying." *This is some kind of sick joke!* Aggravated he fell for it, against his first instinct to stay the course with his treatment and not get involved with anyone, he fumed, *I must've been nuts to think she was for real and could offer help! What the hell's wrong with me, getting sidetracked with this bullshit! I should have known better.*

Stuck in traffic on the ride back to his hotel infuriated him even more as memories surfaced from his last relationship. *I thought I learned from that.* His ex-girlfriend's face came to view, a gorgeous model flashing a smile that enraged him. It was the look she gave him when he found out she'd cheated on him. *How could you laugh it off? Big joke!* He thought of his sullen parents and their whole miserable failed marriage. *Why should I ever expect something more than I've grown up with?*

The emergency room was chaotic with patients on gurneys in the hall, wheelchairs loaded with people, machines buzzing and ringing with patients in various stages of danger. When *code blue* screeched over the intercom, Sara knew she was in for a very long and agonizing wait.

Attempts by the radiology technician to remove Sara's top were met with a deafening "Ow!"

"We're going to have to cut your blouse off." Uneasy about her chest being exposed, she latched onto her top. "Can't you do it with…Oh damn," she remembered Ben.

"I'm sorry about that but I have to get at your arm and chest."

She eyed the technician. "I wasn't reacting to you. I just thought of something else." *Ben—my car—my new outfit destroyed.* "Can you please do me a favor," she winced. "I was supposed to meet someone. He doesn't know I'm here."

"I'm sorry, we're swamped. We need to get you taken care of."

"Please, he's a cancer patient. I don't want to stress him." *I don't want him to think I stood him up.* "Could you make a phone call for me?"

"Have one of the nurses do it when we're finished."

Sara knew from the way everyone was running around, that wasn't going to happen.

"We need to get that top off." He grabbed hold to make the cut.

Sara buckled with every movement of the scissors as each piece of newfound hope was stripped from her. After close to five hours and with no one available to phone Ben, she was brought into a cubicle to be seen by the physician. He walked in holding her X-ray. Gasping, she tried to move air into her strangled chest. "What's the damage?"

"Just a couple cracked ribs."

Just? That's so painful and means no driving for weeks. Morose ideas drowned out what he was saying, until she heard, "Luckily these are simple fractures—the bones are aligned."

It's osteoporosis from the goddamned chemotherapy, and the impact from the air bag alone was enough to do the harm. Oh hell!

"And," he continued, "there's no lung damage."

"That's good."

"I'll have an orthopedic technician come in to tape your ribs and give you aftercare instructions. You can follow up with your own provider. Any questions?"

The rest she already knew—no driving and so on until the swelling and pain were resolved. She didn't want a prescription for medications, Advil would do. Too overwhelmed to think of anything else, "No, thank you."

CHAPTER EIGHT

Ellen arrived at Sara's home shortly after Sara to find her a disheveled mess, lying in bed with Tazzie by her side. "Oh Sara, I'm so sorry. You didn't need to phone a cab. I would have come to get you."

Sara knew that when Ellen heard about her accident, she'd be there for her. They had survived a lot together. Early on, Sara saw the toll it took on Ellen; the dark circles under her eyes told of sleepless nights and worry that her best friend was dying. Ellen's pert frame had held up well through the last two-year ordeal. Their history together, and all Sara had done for Ellen guaranteed loyalty. It wasn't that long ago, just eight years, while Ellen was in an abusive relationship that Sara helped her through a life-changing crisis. Ellen's ex-husband kicked her in the abdomen when she was five months pregnant. Sara found her in the ER hemorrhaging from a ripped uterus necessitating a hysterectomy; the fetus never had a chance. Sara refused to leave her side until Ellen was through the inconsolable grief and court case. This selfless act of loving friendship cemented their bond.

Lackluster, bloodshot eyes cried defeat. "It happened," Sara squirmed in discomfort, "so fast."

Ellen readjusted a pillow to help Sara get more comfortable. "You're going to be okay."

Sinking into the mattress like quicksand, her aching body dead weight, Sara tried to shift position. "Oh, wait a minute, there's something under me." A few minutes of straightening out the sheet to remove wrinkles that felt like knives shooting through her, and she stopped moving.

Touching the reddish discoloration over Sara's arm, "You really got banged up." Ellen sat on the edge of the bed. "What'd they give you for pain?"

"I didn't want any heavy meds," she mumbled.

Seeing how uncomfortable Sara was, "Why not?"

"I've got Advil."

"I know how you struggled with the drugs while on chemo but this is different. You'll let me know if..."

"Yes, I will."

"So, what can I do for you?"

Sara remained quiet, tears raining down onto her bandaged ribs.

Ellen, at a loss for words, reached a hand to Sara's. "I can't believe this after all you've been through."

"Ellen..."

"I'm here."

"Could you phone Ben?"

"Me?" whispered Ellen. "You should do it."

Imploringly looking at Ellen, "I'm uncomfortable..."

"Sara, you can do it and I think it's better if it comes from you. Just pick up the phone." Ellen made a move to get up. "I need to unpack and fix us something to eat."

"I'm not hungry. El, please." Even with a divorce and a few bad memories behind her, she had been strong before the surgery. Daunted by the rib pain, her determination had waned. *I'm deluded to think Ben could ever be interested in me.* Fuzzy glimpses of cobweb images came to mind of a screaming baby until Taz's snoring shifted Sara's attention back to her bedroom. "That's weird."

Ellen gave her a look. "What?"

"My mind's playing tricks. It's probably a spillover from the emergency room."

"Okay then, you going to phone Ben?"

"I'd really rather you did it."

"I know how distressed you are, but I don't want the accident to be a setback. I think talking to Ben would be a good thing, if nothing else a nice distraction to help you heal, but you need to do it."

"Please, El."

"Tell me why you don't want make the call? He's another cancer patient, surely he'll understand." Seeing the vessels on Sara's neck pulsing ferociously, "Talk to me."

"He's going to think I stood him up. I know he's going to be pissed off at me and I don't want to deal with that right now." Another vague image of a crying baby, red-faced from screaming, moved through Sara's head and disappeared.

"Once you explain what happened, you don't think he'll be okay with that?"

"I'm afraid," Sara stuttered.

"Of what?" Ellen's tone softened.

Sara could hardly choke out the word, "rejection." Not feeling accepted was hard for her to experience or speak about. Her ego had built walls of protection, defense mechanisms, to avoid facing the crap she spewed to others about who she was. Were she to confront her self-story, all the nonsense would dissolve into a burning abyss. She deeply feared that if this happened there would be nothing left of her, the identity she had constructed for herself as a nurse and an attractive woman. Without these stories about who she believed she was, all that would remain would be the emotional trauma she'd been hiding from her entire life, and everything she had become would be lost. Without a job, without a partner, without sex, there was nobody there, just pain. She didn't want to face what had started to surface in nightmares. *What are they about? Something happened that makes me feel sick inside.* Nighttime dreams were forgotten and Sara hadn't made the connection between them and the fleeting traces of an unhappy baby that flashed before her in daylight. Crying, a few words emerged. "Not having friends growing up." She cleared her throat to loosen the vise that held it tight. "Being labeled as 'that crazy boy's sister.' I don't want to be labeled. I'm afraid Ben's going to judge and label me."

"Wait a minute, you're not making sense," Ellen interrupted. "Nothing has happened to tell you Ben or anyone else has labeled you anything."

"But…"

"But nothing," said Ellen. "Seriously, you're reacting to the accident and God knows what else. The last thing you need to do is pile a bunch of depressing inaccurate thinking on top of that. You just need to give yourself some time, let things calm down."

"That's probably true, but I want Ben to know why I didn't show."

"Want me to stay here while you do it?"

"Ellen…" Sara pulled up her top to wipe her face. Ellen handed her some Kleenex.

"What, you don't like my snot showing," Sara joked.

"Come on, Sara."

"You know I joke to escape. I don't want a man to look at my body and not find me desirable." Another flash of murky image rose before her, *a fat hand on the baby's leg.* Sara's thighs contracted as the vision dissolved.

Shaking her head in a gesture that said *Stop running*, Ellen looked at Sara inviting her to unfold and communicate what needed to be said without hiding from it any more. "Go on."

Sara blew her nose, glanced at Tazzie, back at Ellen, and spoke pensively. "I think I've always been afraid of abandonment, which is why I was promiscuous when I was a teen. When I had sex, I felt loved. I got what I didn't get at home." She motioned down to her chest. "Who's going to want this?"

"Maybe this stuff with Ben is to trigger these emotions in you. Help you come to terms with some things that you need to deal with." Seeing how wiped out Sara looked, "You know if you really want me to phone him, I will. I don't want you to keep stressing out over…"

"Thank you." Sara eyed her phone. "I don't know what I'd do without you."

"Sara, I just want to do what's best for you. Sometimes that's not easy to figure out."

"What's best for me?" Sara looked at Tazzie's whining and paws twitching in sleep. "Hmm," her attitude lightened, "you're right, El, I should do it."

She grabbed hold of her phone and dialed, but when it went straight to message, she regretted making the move. *My number's going to show! Oh no! Now what?* While his recording sounded and the beep came on, she froze. All that came out was, "Ben, it's Sara. I'm so sorry that I missed meeting…" The machine cut her off with, "If you are satisfied with your message, press one." Flustered, she panicked and pressed it. "Oh shit!" Throwing the telephone down on the bed, "He's going to think I'm the biggest asshole in the…"

"Call him back," Ellen pleaded.

"No!"

Ellen gently moved the cell phone next to Sara's hand.

Seething, Ben arrived back at his hotel mid-afternoon. After leaving a message for Michael, he waited and paced.

"Ben, that's not a smart move. You need to concentrate on your treatment and not get involved with women down there."

"I wasn't getting involved, Mike. I thought it would be something useful. She's been doing well on a study she's on. I wanted to hear about it." Defensively, he continued, "My appointment at Zimmerman's was near there anyway."

"You're at UCLA. There's a whole team networking there and through Zimmerman's office. Don't tell me it's not personal."

Knowing his brother was only watching out for him, this was not what he wanted to hear. "Come on. You're getting all over my case."

Having been in a long surgery, Michael was tired and aggravated. "Hey! Wait a minute here."

"Okay, Mike, calm down."

"I just want you to keep your priorities straight."

Hearing the weariness in his brother's voice, Ben felt foolish that he even bothered phoning him. "You're right. It was stupid of me. It just pisses me off that I fell for it and." He stopped himself. *There's no point in wasting any more time on that flake!*

When he hung up with his brother, Ben saw he had a message.

CHAPTER NINE

Not easily hot under the collar, reading the number made Ben furious. *Who needs this kind of crap!* He deleted the message but couldn't stop thinking of her. Relentless thoughts battered him and the more they came the madder he got. *The gall of someone playing games with a cancer patient!* Still holding the phone when it rang and having half a mind to ignore it, instead he decided to read her the riot act. "You've got a lot of nerve phoning me again!"

Speaking cautiously, hardly above a whisper, "Please, let me explain," Sara pleaded.

"Look, whatever it is you have going on," his jaws clenched, "you need to leave me alone! I suggest you delete…"

"I was in an accident." Pausing to see if he would say something, when he didn't she told him what happened.

He watched the clock on the nightstand flip to a new minute and he knew he had jumped to the wrong conclusion. As he listened to her, his anger melted like snow in sunshine. Usually reticent, this situation with Sara caught him off guard. *I should have tried to reach you to find out.* Subjective assumptions were not how he was used to dealing with things, but then he'd never been diagnosed with a terminal illness before. "Oh, I'm sorry," as he swiped a fly off his leg. "When will you be back at UCLA for your next treatment?"

Scheduled for a blood draw, which she could easily do after if they were to meet, and it wouldn't overly exhaust her, she replied, "Wednesday." *Healing from the injuries, which will be well underway by then, shouldn't interfere with meeting him.*

"How about we meet then?" He watched the insect buzz over to the window, toward the light.

Sara arranged for Ellen to drive and drop her off. She was grateful to Ellen for putting her life on hold to help her when she found out she was ill. Ellen hadn't been involved in a serious relationship for a few years, since she'd broken up with one of the emergency room doctors she was dating. She had tried a couple of online sites but as she ran into less than honest men, she gave up on that. Still skittish from her abusive marriage eight years ago, were it not for Sara's support back then she probably would have completely sworn off men. Ellen was in no hurry to dive into a relationship and being there for Sara, plus her job— she liked working in the emergency room helping frightened, intimidated patients—kept her plenty busy.

Noticing Sara rapidly thumping her foot on the floorboard, "How you doing?"

"I'm all over the place." Sara observed a construction sign on the freeway. "I hope we don't run behind time."

"We've got plenty of time and there's not too much road work ahead."

Not wanting a repeat performance, "I don't want to be late."

"I know," laughed Ellen.

"What's funny?"

"You're going to wear a hole in my car if you keep that up."

Sara instantly stopped moving her foot. "Oh, sorry. Automaticity, burning nervous energy," she grinned.

"It's a brave thing you're doing. Maybe a little foolish," Ellen laughed, "but courageous."

"Maybe a little stupid," Sara returned the laugh, "or a lot stupider."

"Can't wait to hear." The GPS voice indicated a turn into the UCLA parking lot. "As if we hadn't been here a zillion times. I should turn that thing off."

"Yeah, I'd like to turn off a few things as well. I'll ring you in a couple of hours to come and get me." Opening the door, "Don't forget to pick me up by the hematology lab."

"Right, you're having that done today. Okay, have fun and I'll see you then."

Sara headed to the courtyard cafeteria behind the hospital, where they were scheduled to meet. Sweating like a horse, her palms grew clammy, and wiping the unwrapped hand on her pant leg left a mark. *Oh shit, now it looks dirty.* Trying to cover the spot with her purse, she turned a corner and saw him. *I wasn't wrong. He's gorgeous.*

He glanced out from behind circular, lightly-shaded sunglasses. His deep blue eyes met hers and drifted down to her left arm in a sling adhered to her chest with an elastic bandage. "Hi, Sara," he smiled.

Looking down at the mummy wrap, "It's to keep it immobilized." She wondered if he heard the quiver in her voice.

His smooth lips were soft when he spoke. "Here, let me help you." He reached to open the door.

After getting their food, she directed Ben to a quiet shaded place outside, away from foot traffic. "I spent a lot of time here," indicating the exact spot with a head nod, "while in graduate school."

They shared small talk and the time passed with him telling her where he lived and what he did for a job and she explaining her work in the emergency room. "Where'd you go to school?"

"Stanford."

"That's a great school."

"Both my parents and older brother went to Stanford."

Reaching over to the saltshaker, her hand grazed his, sending heat tingling up her spine. "I'm sorry, what'd you just say?"

He found it cute that her cheeks flushed. "My brother is a general surgeon. He practices there."

"That's convenient to have a doctor in the family."

"Yes, it helps. He's a good guy. Too busy though."

Taking a bite out of her bagel, a shadow from a cloud dilated his pupils and she wondered how she looked to him, what he thought of her; she couldn't read his conservative body language. She took a gulp of water, and as the food in her mouth was washed down, so was the self-consciousness she felt with him watching her eat. "What do your parents do?"

"Both are retired. My father was an engineer and my mother an English teacher."

With Ben's attention shifting back to her, Sara thought of her brother Jack but decided not to mention him or her parents. "So tell me, are you comfortable talking about seeing Zimmerman?"

The last thing he wanted to talk about was his illness. "I'm curious to know how your study is going?"

"It's hard to believe it's really happening." *And that I'm here with you.*

He pushed his plate away and listened to what she had to say about the study. "I can understand that." He wiped his mouth with a napkin and thought it interesting that she mentioned cancer but not what type and wondered why.

She noticed he'd left most of his food uneaten.

"I'm happy for your change of luck," he smiled. "Maybe you'll be a lucky charm for me."

His words found her soft spot, the place in her heart that ruled her head. Bursting to touch him, her skin was crawling with desire to feel his body. The sincerity in his responses—not quick, perfunctory, or glib, instead a relaxed thoughtful manner—was a turn-on. "What brought you to him?"

Still not ready to talk about his disease, Ben told her about his brother's connection. "Zimmerman decided to become an oncologist while rooming with Michael."

"Your brother's also named Michael?"

"Yes." Breaking eye contact, deliberating on Zimmerman's decision to specialize in treating cancer patients, he said, "I feel for Zimmerman, what he went through with his own mother. It's why he went into oncology. He was planning on going into family medicine to begin with but then that changed."

"Care to share, if it's not violating any confidences?" Finishing her last bite of food, she was relieved her appetite was back but felt bad for him that his was clearly lacking.

"No, it's fine, he was open about it. His mother died of breast cancer. She was misdiagnosed and mistreated. I don't remember all the specifics but apparently it was a bad scene."

The mention of breast cancer felt like being submerged in a tub of cold water. *He can't tell. Thank God my rib bandage is covering my chest.* "Oh, that's awful." She felt empathy for Zimmerman—who never talked about himself, it wouldn't be appropriate—dealing with cancer patients day in and day out. "I had no idea."

"One of his cousins, a well-known malpractice attorney, told him he had a substantial case for compensation. He refused to go there. He's apparently allergic to our litigious society." He remembered Zimmerman saying, *It wouldn't bring her back.*

"Really? Present company excluded, I'm sure."

"I've never been to court. I'm a paper pusher," Ben joked, "and for the record since I work at NASA, you can call me a civil servant." Returning to a serious mien, "I remember having a conversation with him a long time ago, and his telling me he hated the high cost of medical care." Obviously relieved that the topic was off him personally, Ben continued to relay what he knew about Zimmerman. "He blamed litigation, corrupt billing, and the fear created by pharmaceutical ads on TV that sent hoards of patients to doctors needlessly in search of medication they didn't require."

Sara watched him, how his hands gestured when he spoke, and the way his lips parted inviting sensuality. "Thank you for sharing that with me." She sat up straighter facing Ben. "I'm sorry he went through that with his mother."

Ben nodded agreement.

"He's a rare bird and we're fortunate to have him as our doctor."

"Yes, I really like him."

Toasty from the afternoon sun beating down on her back, Sara realized that they must have been together at least a couple of hours. She wanted to know more about Ben, his diagnosis, prognosis, but when she looked at her watch, it was time to get her lab work done.

"You need to get going?"

"I'm sorry about that. We just barely got started but I have to remember Ellen. My ride. I wish we had more time." What she'd felt moments earlier, the anticipatory thrill over meeting him, their chemistry, was slipping away. *I hope he wants to see me again.*

Feeling an easy affinity with her, a familiarity that he liked, he was disappointed she had to leave. The way the sunlight turned her hazel eyes bright green and lit up her freckled face was a beauty he was captivated by. She reminded him of one of his favorite law school professors; she had helped him make the *Stanford Law Review* and was there for him when no one showed up for his graduation, as Michael had an emergency surgical case that lasted through Ben's ceremony. Seeing Ben alone, she'd offered to take him out for dinner. They developed a friendship—he had meals with her and her lesbian partner, another attorney. She wrote the reference letter that got him the job with NASA, but a few months later they'd drifted apart. Aside from his brother Michael, she was the only person he'd ever met who felt like family. "I was thinking…" He looked at Sara, wrapped up, unable to drive, in her own battle with cancer, and hesitated, wondering if it was a misguided impulse to pursue anything further. "Maybe this isn't a good idea to…" As much as he wanted a connection with her, life taught him to play his cards close to his chest, to keep a safe distance. Up till now this self-protective barrier shielded him, preventing relationships from forming new raw wounds. The news he had advanced cancer cracked that wall.

"Maybe what isn't a good idea?"

Her puppy dog eyes drew him out of any reluctance. "I'd like to see you again," he glanced down at her bandage. "But if you're not up for it, I…"

Trying to calm her enthusiasm, she grabbed for his hand. "I'd really like that."

"Okay, then," he smiled, "I'll call you."

CHAPTER TEN

Ellen could tell the minute Sara got in the car how it went. "So?" She pulled away, listening to Sara gush about Ben for the next hour and a half, along the freeway and back to Ojai. "I'm so happy for you!"

"I just can't believe this is happening to me."

"You deserve it, Sara."

"I don't know about that," Sara smiled, "but I'm not arguing with any of it. I feel so lucky!"

"Good karma."

"You've been hanging around Ojai too long," Sara laughed.

"Speaking of hanging around, do you want me to stay over? I'm off tomorrow."

"You don't need to if you have things to do."

"I do have stuff to take care of." Ellen drove up Sara's driveway.

"See you when you take me for my next appointment."

Taz, sensing Sara's high spirits, ran in circles. "You know girl, don't you?" Sara petted her dog and put on a Rod Stewart CD. On the couch, with Tazzie at her feet, she listened to "A Kiss to Build a Dream On." Tuning in to the words, "So gimme your lips for just a moment and my imagination will make that moment live," her mind went wild. Imagining making love with Ben, what his touch would feel like moving over her thighs, she became aroused. Pumping up the volume, she went to her bedroom.

The next day, floating on air, she puttered around her place and did some reading. But the fortunate turn of events were not to last, for although Sara went to sleep happy at around midnight, she woke up three hours later, wheezing gasps through a cramped torso, like a guppy giving birth to a whale. When streaks of blood clots came up with coughing, she panicked and dialed 911.

With great difficulty she put Taz out back and unlocked the front door for the paramedics. The few minutes it took the ambulance to arrive felt like hours. *My skin feels soggy and is turning blue. Christ, am I having a heart attack? Oh God, I'm so dizzy. It can't be a stroke!* Growing weaker, the black hole of mortality swirled around her in slow motion. *Is it the study I'm on? Please not the cancer!*

The last sound Sara heard before passing out was Taz's barking. She awoke disoriented, unsure of where she was, in an unfamiliar hospital emergency room. Machines filling every available space did nothing to calm her nerves that broke through the sedative fluids running into her arms. Sara felt the prongs in her nose distributing oxygen and saw the concerned expression on an aide hovering as she slurred, "Where am I?" before blacking out again.

Coming to in a private room in the Intensive Care Unit, a nurse adjusting one of her intravenous lines said, "You're awake."

"What…"

"You're at UCLA." The woman told Sara that she was stabilized in an ER in Ventura County and, "Zimmerman had you transferred here because of the study you're on." She finished straightening the tube in Sara's arm. "That way you'll be monitored by the physicians on the research team." She explained that a pulmonary embolism had dislodged and settled in her lungs, making it difficult for her to breathe. "We think it's from your recent auto accident." Her medical records had been faxed there when she arrived, including the ER visit after the auto crash. "Clot busting and anticoagulant medications were given just in time and nothing further needs to be done other than keep an eye on you for a couple of days."

"I've never had a problem with clots." Sara, still groggy, was lucid enough to know her history. "I've been in accidents and never..."

"It could be the aftermath from the chemo you were on before, and it can also be a side effect of the treatment you're on now. That's one of the reasons you're here, so they can watch you. At any rate you're in good hands and are going to be okay."

Sara worried that it might be more than the recent injury or a drug adverse reaction. Her neck muscles tensed into a stranglehold. "I didn't think a pulmonary embolism was a side effect of the meds I'm on."

"Correct, but lung swelling is." The nurse was distracted by the beeping from one of the monitors, and after making a slight adjustment continued, "And while it's still in trial phases, it's unknown what can show up."

Lung swelling! Sara knew along with coughing up blood, the hoarseness she heard in her voice, and now neck pain, swelling could be an indication that cancer was in her lungs. "I'm assuming they did a scan to diagnose this?"

"Yes, and it showed nothing other than the embolism."

"They're sure," Sara's stomach twisted, "the swelling isn't from a new growth?"

The nurse nodded, "Yes, that's what the radiology report said." Injecting Ativan, she smiled, "You're going to be okay."

Not convinced, Sara echoed, "They didn't see any new tumor?"

On finishing the infusion, "I read the report, and…" the nurse clamped the line to prevent air from entering and wiped the port with alcohol, "there's no mention of anything else. The only reason you're here is to be sure there isn't some complicating factor from the research drug you're on. There's been absolutely no indication in your chart that any new growths have been seen."

Doubt was written all over Sara's face.

"Your lungs are clearing, indicating the swelling is reducing. That wouldn't be happening if a mass was the problem." Moving the sheet up over Sara's chest, "Now you need to rest."

Reassurance from the nurse eased the tangles in Sara's muscles while the fluids took effect, and she stopped caring about why she'd thrown a clot. As her breathing calmed she was able to comfortably inhale the air-conditioned breeze of disinfectant diffusing through the atmosphere, covering up disease and death. Antiseptic perfume flowed into her widened nostrils and she thought about what Tazzie would smell were she here. Having read about dogs finding cancers in samples of urine, she wondered if Taz sniffed out hers to begin with. "I need to phone my friend," she slurred, "to watch my dog."

As the chemicals permeated her body, she drifted off. *A fat grotesque freak with big hands loomed over the baby's crib. Drool dripped from his jaws. He's going to do something. Something terrible. Admonitions from someone else scared him off. The voice came closer and there was a pressure on the baby's shoulder.* Disoriented, Sara opened her eyes to see a blur of Rosalie standing over her. "What's happening?" Confused about what she was seeing, she shut her eyes but the nightmare had evaporated. She felt a firm hand on her shoulder.

"Sara," her father broke through her daze, "we're here."

Sara saw her father, "I've…been…dreaming?" Remembering where she was, she looked back and forth at her parents. "Hi," she mumbled.

"So," Rosalie looked around the room at the intravenous machine, the monitor flashing a pulse and blood pressure, and a device on Sara's finger, "you got some sleep in this noise?"

Jolted from the edge in her mother's tone, Sara was wide awake. The look on her father's face, sagging distressed wrinkles of clay, was no help either. "Dad, I'll be fine. It's not the cancer." Irving's feigned smile didn't hide the heartache she knew he must have been feeling over seeing her looking so fragile. "Please don't…"

"I'm okay. You just get yourself well. You're my life. It's probably not from the study you're on."

Rosalie barged in, "I told you not to get your hopes up." She looked down at Sara. "They said they think it's from that accident you were in. When are you going to learn to drive slower and…"

Irving nudged her to shut up.

Sara wished they would leave. Carefully, she expressed to her parents, "It would be better for everyone if you could take care of Tazzie so Ellen would be able to work and visit me in the hospital." She wanted her best friend, another experienced nurse, by her side. What she couldn't say was she didn't want to stress her father, and she could do without her mother's comment about needing to drive more carefully.

Rosalie grumbled, "Your friend, instead of your mother? Your parents?"

Sara wanted to take the lines running into her arms and shove them down her mother's throat.

"Of course, we'll stay at your place." Irving shot Rosalie a look that said, *No more!* "Where's Ellen now?"

"She's working. She'll be here first thing tomorrow."

"But…" Rosalie sputtered.

Irving took hold of Rosalie. "We'll let you rest now."

Ellen arrived the following morning with a few personal things, including Sara's purse. "I'm relieved I'm off for the next three days. Your coloring's good. You look much better than I expected."

Appearing unruffled, Sara said, "Yeah, I think I'm doing okay. What a trip."

"They took off your rib bandage?"

"Yes, I don't need to wear it while I'm here. It'll go back on when I'm discharged."

"Any discomfort there?"

"As long as I don't move too much, it's okay."

"This was so unexpected."

Sara motioned to her handbag. "Thanks for bringing my phone. Any messages?"

"Nothing."

"Oh," moaned Sara.

"Give it time. It's only been two days since you've seen him."

"Could you please call him to let him know what happened?"

"Sure."

Early the next morning, a nurse holding a clipboard entered Sara's room. "Hello Sara," she said as she moved to the side of the bed. Nodding to the name badge pinned to the lab coat she was wearing, "I'm Catherine, one of the nurses on the research project you're on."

"I haven't seen you around there," Sara commented.

"No, you wouldn't have. I don't administer the medication. I'm behind the scenes running the project," she smiled.

Just then Sara's parents arrived and Rosalie flew off the handle at Catherine. "You the one who phoned us at ten..."

Taken aback, "Huh?" responded Catherine.

"Then it wasn't you? Who phones in the middle of the night? I want to know who..."

Puzzled, "What's going on?" asked Sara.

Rosalie moved closer. "They wanted us here to be with you..." and drawn out for melodramatic effect, she droned, "to discuss a serious question."

Rosalie's tone gave Sara a fright. "What!"

Catherine jumped in. "It's nothing to be alarmed about. There's just a question with the trial drug and a medication you've been started on since being admitted. We need an informed consent signed."

Sara shot her mother a look. Then back to Catherine, "What's the situation?"

"We had a meeting last night with the research team and your doctors to discuss this." Catherine went on to explain the dilemma. The concern was, could Sara be on an anticoagulant safely, or should they drop her from the research project. She looked around to everyone in the room and solemnly continued, "If we stop the chemo, you're back to where you started. If you're on the anticoagulant, there's risk of bleeding if…"

Sara was steadied by Catherine's gentle, compassionate manner. "Have there been any women on the study who've also been on blood thinners? If so, were there complications with any of them? Problems with bleeding?" Sara wiped beads of sweat from her forehead. "Anything specific I should know about?"

"No. Luckily there have been women who have been through the study and were on Coumadin, the medication you are taking. They came through without any problems. Ultimately the choice is up to you and since the study is ongoing with the admission criteria intact, and this didn't violate or go against it, there's no further conflict with the team. But, and this is where the potential risk is, since it's still in the investigative stages, we don't know all the possible side effects."

"They had to sign consents to stay on the Coumadin?"

"Yes."

"And," looking at her father, regretting what she had to say, "if I don't take chemo, I have maybe a couple of months to live?"

The nurse nodded.

Irving's mouth dropped open, "I thought she was coming along so well with the study."

Seeing the pained expression on her father's face, Sara interrupted, "Can you just explain the situation briefly."

"The research drug works fast but once stopped," Catherine turned from Sara to Irving, "the aggressive nature of your daughter's cancer can exacerbate and undo what the trial has achieved."

Sara had heard enough. "Okay, let's do it. Where's the paper?"

Catherine added, "We need your parents to witness this, which is why we brought them in." Sara's squinting a perplexed look prompted Catherine to continue, "Ativan— if there's any question with your being alert to understand what you're signing."

"Mind-altering drugs? CYA," smiled Sara.

"How about speaking English," Rosalie rolled her eyes.

"Cover your ass. Translates to they need to protect themselves from litigation," Sara coughed. "The drug I'm on can impact how I'm thinking."

Rosalie muttered, "Why can't people learn to speak English."

With the signatures obtained, Catherine left Sara with her parents. Narrowing her eyes, Rosalie said, for what seemed like the thousandth time, "You need to drive more carefully." Smacking her lips, "When are you ever going to learn?"

Wanting to lash out and kick her mother away, like a swimmer pulled under by a shark, spasms of anger grabbed her already sore muscles and Sara wanted to holler, *I'm so sick of your bullshit!*

After lunch, Ellen found Sara alone.

"Did you get hold of him?"

"No, I just left a message."

"What'd you say?"

"I told him I was your ride when you guys met for lunch, that you were here and you wanted me to let him know."

Sara slumped back onto her pillow, "I hope he phones."

"So do I." Ellen pulled up a chair, "You look worn out."

"Rosalie," letting out a loud groan, "she's so obnoxious with her 'I told you so' attitude and dramatics. Drives me up the wall. I wish she'd never heard it could have been from the accident. She's all over my case about how I drive. I felt like saying, 'I was only going five miles per hour!' Not exactly what I need."

"She's such a pain! Does she ever let up?"

"You've been my friend for how many years now?" Sara's words blurred by exhaustion, "You be the judge."

"On to something more pleasant." Ellen held up an iPod. "I brought this. Let's put on some songs and we can relax together."

By the time the first tune started, Sara was fast asleep.

CHAPTER ELEVEN

The aroma of breakfast sent heart rates into calmer zones on the floor that Sara had been transferred to the night before. Unlike most other hospitals, UCLA is a state-of-the-art facility that caters to its celebrity clientele and patients with good food.

The nurse brought in the breakfast tray, which was unusual. But the minute Sara looked down and saw the small teddy bear wearing a UCLA t-shirt, she understood. "You have a special admirer. And he's very cute. He didn't want to interrupt your meal and," she put the food down on the over-bed table, "said he'd be back later."

Sara's heart flipped over in anticipation as she searched for a note. It was taped to the backside and said "See you soon." No signature. It wasn't needed. *I can't believe he did this.* She burst into tears.

"Oh no," the nurse squinched her face, "I'm sorry. Is he someone you didn't want..."

"Not..." Sara could hardly speak.

Confused, the nurse handed her a tissue.

"Not at all," Sara wiped her tears dry. "I'm happy."

"That's a relief," the nurse laughed.

Sobbing turned to laughter. The outpour was a purge of shock upon shock of bad news—from the chemo and radiation therapy, multiple emergency room admissions, her mother's attitude and father's health, worry over what would happen to Tazzie, and countless sleepless nights and worrisome days, one after the other.

The nurse waited a few seconds before saying, "I'll be back later to give you your meds."

Adding cream and sugar, the coffee looked like a latte—her favorite drink. Steam rose from the cup, along with images reminding her of Henry. Some of their happiest times together were going out to a coffee house and listening to jazz.

They met while she was an undergraduate in the nursing program and married shortly after, when he was out of school and working. It seemed too good to be true, until he came across a new movement founded on ideas generated by Descartes. At first it made sense to her but as the group became demanding, overpowering, insisting they donate time and money to sustain its principles, she dared to question its tenets. The consequences were devastating; he chose the group over her when she was excommunicated.

She waved her head in an effort to rid it of him, questioning if it was even possible. The bad taste of the humiliating embarrassment lessened as she sipped coffee and cuddled the gift from Ben.

Sara supported a mirror against the water pitcher to put on makeup and comb her hair. She tried to busy herself with a magazine to no avail as her excitement grew with every set of footsteps moving down the hallway. A few false alarms of staff entering the room intensified her jitters, while she redid lipstick and blush. Relieved when Ellen arrived, she exclaimed, "I'm going nuts."

"You're glowing. I'd say it's more than the medicine making you happy." Pointing at the stuffed animal, Ellen smiled, "Is that from…"

"Yes!" muffled Sara.

"How cute." She picked it up and read what he wrote. "That's why the rouge and gloss?"

"Uh-huh."

When Ben arrived an hour later to find them talking, Ellen stood to greet him. Extending a hand, "You must be Ben." A glance at him and Ellen instantly shot Sara a smiling look.

Sara read Ellen like an open book. The validation showing in Ellen's body language sent Sara soaring. *I told you he was gorgeous!*

Ellen pointed to the seat, "Here, make yourself comfortable, I need to get going."

"Please don't go on my account." He waited to see if Ellen would sit.

"Oh, no really I do" Ellen eyed Sara, "need to run some errands," and sauntered out.

Ben turned his attention to Sara and saw the contusions from needle sticks in her arms and hands, the multiple attachments she had to an intravenous machine, and the sheet pulled up to her neck. Wincing, he tried to cover up his concern with a sympathetic smile. "You don't look too bad. I was expecting worse."

Sara picked up the teddy bear and hugged it to her chest. "Thank you so much for this."

"I thought you'd appreciate the little guy." He sat down.

She watched him move, and the way the wrinkles in his dark blue jeans puckered.

"This is quite an institution," his smile stiffened. "It's a hike to get around here. I'm glad I'm staying a couple of blocks away and don't have to worry about a parking space."

She saw through the cheerful mask to his drawn face and wondered, *What are you holding back?* She was familiar with covering up her feelings to present an acceptable front, because we don't just come to the party and respond, *I feel like shit*, to the usual, *How you doing?* She worried it might be personal, that his visit could bring bad news. "How are you, Ben?"

He tried to hide that he didn't relish talking about his treatment. Not wanting to be a downer, especially with all she had been through, he responded, "Doing okay. So tell me, how are they treating you here?"

She took his lead and dropped prodding any further. "No complaints. I better not," she laughed. "I know too many people who work here. One of my classmates from grad school came to see me last night when she got off duty."

"Where does she work?"

"Peds."

"Oh, that'd be a tough floor to work. I doubt I'd be useful around sick kids. Or animals," he broke eye contact. "That's my Achilles heel."

"Animals!"

"You like them too?"

Tazzie's whole sordid history came out. "On some of my worst days, she was there and perked me up. You'll have to meet her. She's little for a rottie and..." Catching herself from getting too wordy, she slowed the pace. "I'm sorry, I'm getting way ahead of myself. I don't even know what your plans are or how long you'll be here."

"Sounds like Tazzie's a good friend," as he veered from mention of his treatment timeline. "Dogs usually are." A nurse who entered to administer medication through the

IV line interrupted Ben. Waiting for her to finish, he asked, "Giving you the choice stuff?"

"Not this time. That was my blood thinner." Motioning to the bruises on her arms, "How do you like my art work?"

"Van Gogh has nothing on you," he laughed. "You look good to me."

The once-over he gave her sent her stomach into flips. A giddy flush moved over her as the hospital noise and commotion disappeared in a burst of elation. She didn't remember hearing much of the small talk they made back and forth before he noticed her eyelids start to get droopy. "I don't want to tire you. I better be heading out for now."

"You don't have to."

"You need your rest, Sara." He stood and gave her face a gentle caress. "Take care of yourself."

When Ellen returned, Sara was up out of bed sitting in the chair, looking radiant. "I'm going home tomorrow."

CHAPTER TWELVE

Sara had been out of the hospital, feeling better and regaining strength, for a week. Along with her improving health came more fantasizing over Ben. She had spoken with him several times in light conversations about books they liked to read, movies, politicians they could do without, and how her healing was coming along. She frequently observed how adept he was at deflecting questions concerning his health.

Ben's attention to Sara was encouragement that he was interested in her. Little comments about her "cute smile" or "inviting eyes" helped her to feel attractive, intensifying her yearning to be with him. But as the phone conversations continued, she was relieved that their getting together was delayed until she gave him the green light. The cloud on the horizon of their union was conflicting emotions that were equally strong: her fear of exposing her naked body to him and the unrelenting desire to make love with him—to feel like a complete woman. As her feelings battled, her trepidation over how it would play out increased. *Am I fooling myself? He's a man. They're visual creatures. But maybe he likes me enough.*

Resting comfortably with her ribs still taped, there were no further complications with her lungs or bruising from the medication. With Ellen taking care of her and Tazzie shadowing, she was relieved to be home.

As she lay in bed watching the overheard light dangle on the ceiling, the swaying shadow mesmerized her. Listening to Tazzie's guttural sounds, asleep next to her, she remembered back to when she first saw her at the shelter. Taz's file stated she came from a puppy mill in

Arkansas and was shipped cross country and sold in a pet shop in Santa Monica, California. The couple who purchased her had her for a few weeks before she ran into the street and was hit by a truck. They dumped her into the kill shelter with a broken femur. Three days before she was to be euthanized, Sara went there to walk the dogs, as she did every week. She met Tazzie, whose leg was splinted, and brought her home. "I love you, Tazzie girl," Sara whispered. "Maybe soon you'll have a new buddy. His name is Ben and he told me, 'You sound like a good friend.' He's so right. You're the best. I know you'll like him."

Taz's gentle rhythmic snoring lulled Sara. Soon she drifted off to sleep. *The beast trudged closer to the baby's crib. His fat hand reached down to lift up the blanket. The baby was frantic. A voice told him to leave her alone. Holding his ears to make it stop, he looked around the room and smiled; he was alone with the hysterical baby.*

Taz, turning onto her back, jerked Sara awake. Heart pounding in her chest, she scanned the room to get her bearings. *Why is this happening now, when I'm starting to feel better? Ommmm.* She tried to direct her attention to the mantra she used during meditation, to no avail. *What are these dreams all about? Ommmm.* Her heart rate slowed. *Am I afraid to be with Ben?* Her body shivered. *Ommmm. Am I scared I'll look deformed to him?* Fragments of the nauseating nightmare faded away.

Ellen entered holding a cup of tea. "I brought you..." One look at Sara's face, "You okay?"

"Another bad dream." Sara held up her right hand, "I'm still shaking."

"You're covered in sweat." Ellen felt Sara's forehead with the back of her hand.

"I don't feel warm."

"You don't have a fever. Let me get you a washcloth."

After wiping herself, "That's much better," she handed the cloth back to Ellen. "Thanks."

Ellen sat on a rocking chair next to the bed. "Want to talk about anything?"

"It's weird, El." Attempting to clear a few strands of wet hair off her forehead, "Ow," she pulled her hand back. Shifting to a comfortable position to ease the muscle spasms in her shoulder, "These horrible visions! One of them was a big fat monster. It reminded me of Jack."

"Your brother?"

"Yes."

"Hmm, wonder what that's about," responded Ellen.

"Probably just my mind playing tricks. But it felt so real." Sara became thoughtful.

"Think out loud. It might help."

"I wondered if it was my insecurity over being with Ben, but they started shortly after I was diagnosed, way before I met him."

"The shock from finding out could have initially triggered it." Still in her hand, Ellen squeezed the cool, moist cloth. "We go along coping nicely, with our hidden trauma neatly packed away until something enters and throws the dirty laundry all over the place."

"And what's this have to do with a terrified baby? I can't make any sense out of these nightmares."

"What exactly did you dream?"

"I don't really remember. I just have this very uncomfortable feeling about them."

"Do you think it would help if you talked to someone?"

"I am," laughed Sara, "talking to someone. But no, that doesn't feel right to me. It helps just telling you."

"You do look better."

"El..."

Ellen swayed back and forth in the rocking chair. "Uh-huh."

"What would I do without you?" A warm comfortable bath of gratitude surged through Sara's body, replacing remnants of the mysterious darkness. "I don't know how to thank you."

"You just did."

Sara's eyes got teary.

"Sara, you're the best friend I've ever had and we're in this together, till you're healed."

"From your mouth to God's ears."

"Yes," Ellen stood. "If you don't need anything else I'll put this wet cloth away and finish making dinner."

Sara's thoughts went to Ben and how he was doing. She wanted to know about his treatment. Hearing the weariness in his voice when they were on the phone, the jittery stutters through the laughter, it bothered her that she knew so little about him. She rationalized, *He'll be okay. I know I was a mess.* The attraction she felt for him as a woman overrode her intuition as a nurse, and she convinced herself that if she felt as good as she did, *He has to be okay. It'll work out.* Issues she'd had with abandonment took a back seat to her overpowering need for intimacy. Hopeful affirmations about being with him calmed the ambivalence, throwing caution to the wind. *It will be okay! Ben, you didn't arrive in my life at this time for me to lose you. We were meant to be together. Why else would I want you so much?*

Zimmerman phoned Ben to say he wanted to add something to his regime. He had read a study done at the University of Bern, Switzerland, where mistletoe extract was injected subcutaneously twice a week in patients with advanced ductal pancreatic carcinoma. Of great benefit was the fact that no severe side effects were observed.

"When do you want to start?" asked Ben.

"You can start today. Can you get over to my office? I'll do it here a couple of times a week on the days it doesn't conflict with your treatment at UCLA."

"I can't have it done there?"

"It's not on their protocol so they can't administer it."

Ben's mouth turned dry. "Will it interfere with the other drug, the treatment I'm getting there?"

"No, it shouldn't."

Ben flashbacked to his conversation with Sara about her being started on Coumadin and having to sign papers and thinking she was cavalier to go forward. Now faced with a decision that might save his life, he understood the choice she made and why. Feeling it was the right way to go didn't stop the visceral angst. "If it's not on their protocol," he faltered, "I won't be taken off the study, will I?"

"No. It's my study and I wrote a clause into it that covers me administering things at my office. UCLA can't do it unless they get the okay for that specific medication, and the paperwork red tape would take too long. I want to get you started right away. That's the only reason we're not doing it there."

"Okay then, it's Tuesdays and Fridays at your office?"

"Yes."

On his way to Zimmerman's he thought of Sara, how she looked when he last saw her. Stirring a tenderness in him that no woman had done before, it hit a sensitive nerve to see her so helpless. *I'd like to see her again.* Wanting to phone her, *I don't know how I'm going to feel after the injection,* he opted to wait.

Chapter Thirteen

Zimmerman's waiting room was crowded, a solemn reminder to Ben that his doctor had a lot more patients to worry about than him. Ben wondered what their stories were, especially the teenage boy sitting beside his mother, who kept telling him to sit up straight. The poor kid, jaundiced, looked like hell. Another, a sixtyish woman, sat with nothing covering her bald head.

Lost in thoughts of what his chances might be, he became distracted by a woman who entered wearing heavy perfume that permeated the suite. Resisting the sickening odor, he was relieved when the nurse called his name and took him to the treatment room.

Zimmerman entered, carrying some papers that he handed to Ben. "Here's the study for you to have a look at."

Hopeful until he glanced down at the highlighted part that said, "can stabilize quality of life in their few remaining months," apprehension hit him hard. What he expected would be good news took him by surprise. Any hope that mistletoe extract would afford him years was a joke. Aggravated that he'd agreed to commit to twice a week, "That's it? That's all this is about?"

"Ben," Zimmerman, having not seen any dramatic improvement in Ben's lab work since he started the study, paused, "we have to consider the data, be receptive to change if..." He broke eye contact and looked pensive, like he didn't know what to say, then, "Ben, I wish I could tell you I might be wrong, or even that miracles happen, but I don't want to mislead you. I wish it were different. I'm so sorry."

Ben knew there was no escaping into denial and that if the study at UCLA had helped he wouldn't be here now receiving something that only offered comfort for the little time he ostensibly had left. *Months? That can't be right. But that's what it said.* Feeling the dampness under his arms, he wished he could turn back the clock to before his first abdominal pains, which he thought were just something he ate or gas pangs. Then he could look forward to more than a bundle of weeks; there would be years ahead and a future filled with plans. The one question he hadn't asked that he feared the answer to crept into his head. No reprieve was possible till he coughed out, "What's your best guess? What're we talking about here?"

Zimmerman squared his shoulders. "Look, you're my best friend's brother and this isn't easy to say, especially to you. I'm in this job to keep people alive, not give them news that drains the hope out of their eyes, but sometimes I have to. This is one of those times. Your prognosis isn't good. Maybe six months. I'm sorry, Ben."

Ben's stomach rose to his throat. "Oh shit!" Turning pale and clammy, Zimmerman had him put his head down between his knees.

"Ben, I can check around to see if there are any new studies starting." To Ben, it sounded like his doctor was bordering on platitude, yet aware he should switch gears and refocus back on what may offer relief, so he listened with a dull mind while Zimmerman said, "Maybe Johns Hopkins, Mayo Clinic, Memorial Sloan-Kettering, or MD Anderson will have something. If not directly, they are the best cancer centers in the states and will be tapped into the international scene."

Ben was aware that if there were something, Zimmerman would have presented it to him. Since nothing other than the offering that came with little chance of benefit was all there was, he muttered, "I don't believe this." He stared out the window beyond Zimmerman's office to the large hospital complex and thought of patients in there on their last legs who had received similar news. Hearing a tumble of words coming out of his doctor's mouth, nothing made any sense to his dizzy head.

Still, Zimmerman persisted. "Keep a positive focus. Make the best of every moment." When Ben didn't bother to respond, "Ben, don't give up on living."

Living! That word collided into Ben, like a strike in bowling, jolting him out of his funk. The slippery slope into a morose hell, thoughts of nothing left for him to look forward to or be alive for except what the cancer would bring—that future brought nothing aside from a painful headache. *Alive, that's how I feel with Sara.* He knew there was something about her that he couldn't put his finger on till now. *You make me feel alive. A lot of healthy people walk around blankly staring into space but no one's home. There you are battling with cancer and those eyes of yours are lit up. Sara!* The room suddenly brightened when he saw, *Right now I'm okay, alive, functioning well, and no one knows what tomorrow will bring, no guarantees for anyone.*

Ben realized that what's important, as Zimmerman brought home to him, is living. He'd never fully understood the power of a positive attitude until this moment, when the chemistry inside him shifted—dissolving adrenaline and stress hormones—to allow his body to relax. Oddly, he thought of the last time he was at Lake Tahoe with the sun beating down on his back, listening to boats rippling on the water, inhaling fresh air, watching birds drift along with the cumulus clouds. He knew what it felt like to be alive, then and now. *I'll be damned if I'm going to let whatever is left of my life slip away. Who the hell knows what's in store for me anyway?* "You're absolutely right. I need to stop dwelling in tomorrow and what I think will happen and just pay attention to where I'm at currently. No guarantees for any of us for what's going to occur in the next hour. This is definitely a shift in big picture perspective," Ben smiled. "Thanks, I'll do the injections here and anything else you think will help one way or another."

Zimmerman heaved an audible sigh. "I'm glad that you had a change of heart and agree to stay the course with the program. And it's true what you said, no guarantees. And no one, including me, can predict the future with total certainty."

CHAPTER FOURTEEN

Chicken with mushrooms baked in the oven as Tazzie's snout sniffed upward. Ellen, ignoring the dog's whining, continued to prepare dinner. Taz sat still, staring a thick intention into Ellen's every move. When the whimpering failed, the dog nudged Ellen's hand.

Ellen, laughing at the persistence, "You just ate," headed for the dog cookie jar.

Taz's golden eyes were fixed on the prize.

"Here!" Ellen threw her a treat. "Now stop bugging me." As she washed her hands, she heard an outcry. Taz sprang out, followed by Ellen who made it to Sara's bedroom short-winded. "What happened?"

"I don't believe it!" Sara, beside herself with exhilaration, said, "He called!"

"Okay, and that means what? You've been talking to him all week."

"Ben's coming over here!"

"That's great. Stop shouting and tell me when?"

"Now! He's coming now!"

Ellen went back to the kitchen and added more chicken to the meal, while Sara slowly maneuvered herself to get ready.

When the phone rang, Sara's first thought was Ben had changed his mind. Instead, the number was Rosalie's. "Oh crap!" She knew if she didn't pick up her mom would phone every five minutes until she did. Anxious that Ben would be arriving any minute, unsure what else to do, she answered. "Mom, hold on a minute, will you?" She went to the kitchen to have Ellen put Taz outside and intercept Ben when he got there.

On hearing it was Rosalie calling, "Oh shit, lousy timing," Ellen pulled a face. "Don't worry I'll handle..."

Back in contact with her mother, Sara girded her loins. Not having seen her parents since being released from the hospital, she could well imagine what she was in store for. "Okay, sorry mom."

"What kept you?"

"I had to let Taz out."

Rosalie, sounding constipated, forced out, "So, how are you?"

"Healing nicely, mom. How's everything your end? Dad?"

"He has his good days and bad days. You know how it is," was her usual no-answer response.

"So listen, mom, El's making dinner and I need to get ready to eat. Can I get back to you tomorrow?"

"We thought we'd drive up tomorrow."

Bad timing! I may be too tired.

The ring of the doorbell, sending adrenaline pumping to Sara's already nervous stomach, vied for her attention. *I hope to God she can't hear it.* Words stuck in her throat. "I have friends coming from the emergency room, staying the night. It'd be too much..." she lied.

"Too much to have your parents there in that big house of yours?"

The disgust in Rosalie's voice hooked into Sara, sucking away the joy she'd felt moments earlier. She abhorred the effect her mother had on her, the utter lack of control to let it pass. *Not now, damn it!* Wanting to slam the phone down, she flashbacked to the last time she hung up on her mother, which took weeks to repair.

Calm down before answering. Don't let her get the better of me. Breathe.

"Well?" Impatiently, Rosalie continued, "We'll see you…"

No! "Mom, I want to see you, but I need to take it slowly, please…"

Silence.

Sara didn't know what was worse, the cold shoulder or the caustic attitude that made her feel unloved and small. "Mom?" She twisted her bedspread into a ball she wanted to throw out the window.

"Go eat your dinner," carped her mother before the line went dead.

Why now? Mood deflated, like an inner tube with a leak, she wanted to release the exasperation howling in her brain. *Why! What the hell is wrong with you!* The worst part of it was the heartache, craving a relationship she desperately wanted—a mother she could talk to and be close with.

Still out of kilter from that conversation, Sara attempted to regain composure by looking around the room focusing on objects there. When that didn't help, she grabbed the stuffed elephant on the bed, and felt the imprints where she had held it in the past for comfort and security. *This instead of you!* Her mother was always at a guarded distance away from arm's reach, too far for hugs. She squeezed its soft belly as tears welled up, until commotion in the other room between Ben and Tazzie summoned her.

CHAPTER FIFTEEN

Blinking away residual tears, Sara wiped her face and made her way to the laughter, toward the aroma of food, out of the dark bedroom to the light dining area where large French doors let in the sunshine. She found Ben on the floor being licked to death by her dog, and Ellen in the kitchen finishing up the meal.

Looking up to Sara, Ben rubbed Tazzie's shoulders. "Vicious rottweiler," he smiled.

"Yeah, she's the devil incarnate."

Taking a closer look, he noticed her red puffy eyes and stood up. "You okay?" With the backdrop of her bandaged ribs, her vulnerability in the hospital, and how authentically friendly she was when they lunched together, he felt himself softening.

Ellen spoke up from the kitchen, "Her mother!" Sprinkling seasoning on the rice, "Oh yeah, I invited Ben for dinner."

Ellen's exclamatory remark about Sara's mother caught Ben's attention. He'd been thinking of his own childhood, none of it pleasant. Although he wondered if they had an unhappy upbringing in common, it wasn't something he wanted to broach with her.

"I'm okay now," Sara motioned to the step-down living room. "Want me to show you around?"

Lots of windows afforded him a view of the park-like property with a creek running through it. "Sara, this is a great place. You have redwoods?" He looked at one of the trees, the needles turning brown.

"I think it was a transplant." Sadly discouraged, "Some aren't doing that well in the warm climate and drought we've been having. I hope they make it."

"I hope so too."

She walked him out to the front deck of her rustic country house. "Considering how little rainfall we've had this year, there's still a lot of bloom."

"You planted these?" he asked, referring to the overgrowth of a colorful array of geraniums, and Matilija poppies.

"Yes." Interrupted by a coyote barely visible, running down the side of the property, "Look," she whispered.

Ben's sight moved toward two squirrels that sensing danger, froze. The wild dog was ready to lunge when Ben clapped his hands and frightened it off. "It's a good day when you can save a life."

"He'll find dinner somewhere else." Watching it disappear into the culvert in the creek, "I know it happens but hate to see it."

"Same here. Oh look," he pointed, "they're wagging their tails, saying thanks."

"Good thing Tazzie's inside."

"Yeah, something about dogs and squirrels," he laughed.

Embracing the natural environment she lived in, he couldn't imagine a better place to be. Appreciating the shift he'd had at Zimmerman's, *Moment to moment is how to live*, he looked at Sara, the alluring fluidity of her movement, how the sun constricted her pupils accentuating the glow of her hazel irises. *I'm so glad I phoned you.*

Back in the house he caught the scent of lavender from an aromatherapy lamp. "You like pottery," referring to a row of vases and bowls by the hearth.

"Yes," she smiled, "from Ojai's very own. I like to support the local community. We've a lot of terrific artists here. That elephant painting," she pointed to the large oil over the couch, "is from a favorite painter who lives in town." Remembering the stuffed animal in her bedroom, "I can't get enough of them. I have several," she pointed to the bookshelves with bronze and sandstone pachyderms. "Someone told me they're my totem animal, and that when an elephant appears, it's watching over me. I figured out why not have that insurance—ergo the painting and herd," she laughed.

"Totem animal? That's an American Indian tradition, isn't it? Elephant, huh?"

"I do know that totems are found in the history of other than American Indian cultures. And yes, Native American Indians do believe that animals enter and leave our lives depending on our needs, guiding us. I thought it odd that he said elephant but I didn't query it." Catching a questionable look on his face, *Oh cripes, I don't want to come across airy-fairy.* "Not that I believe it. I'm not into believing much of anything, but I think the Indians possess a lot of wisdom. They are more in touch with the earth than anyone I've met."

Fascinated by her comment, "You've spent time around them?"

The accepting tone in his voice lessened the resistance she felt that he might be judging her because she referred to something elusive. "Professionally, yes, I had that privilege of doing a clinical rotation with a tribe. They welcomed and made me feel like family. It was very fulfilling."

"I'm not much into believing things either but I agree with you about the wisdom of these people. Their heritage shows a deep respect for living off and with the land. My own love of nature and animals makes it easy for me to imagine that it would be very rewarding to connect with them."

Ellen yelled from the kitchen, "Dinner!"

They made their way to the steaming dishes. "How nice," Ben pulled out a chair, "of you to do this."

"My pleasure."

"So," Ben asked, "how'd you two meet?"

Ellen made small talk about how she met Sara. Seeing he was pushing the food around on his plate and not eating much, she joked, "I know I'm not the best cook."

Sara nudged Ellen's foot under the table. "Ben, just eat whatever you want. We understand."

Ellen blushed and switched the topic. "Sara told me you went to Stanford?"

Ben let out a long breath, "Yeah, I'm a Cardinal diehard," and took a courteous bite of chicken.

"Nineteen-seventy was a good year for the red and white." Ellen flashed a redeemed grin. "Are you impressed I know about your football team?" Seeing Sara was confused, "It's the only time Stanford took the Heisman Trophy home." Ellen shot Ben a look that said gotcha.

"Don't be so smug, you guys only took it once."

"We've had more than one," protested Ellen.

Ben sat up straighter, "Nope, friend, just Beban."

"You're sure?"

"You've turned out dozens of NFL players but Gary Beban is the only Heisman winner." Jokingly, he smirked, "My Cardinal minor was football."

"I didn't know that." Cutting a piece of meat, Sara said, "I'm not really into football, but El is."

The conversation continued while Ben, not wanting to draw attention to his lack of appetite, forced himself to shovel down more food.

Watching him slowly move his hands and the way his lips parted, Sara fantasized about what it would be like to be with him. Stirrings in her body stopped when she saw him look at the kitchen clock that was approaching eight.

"Well, this has been great, you two. Glad I phoned but I'd better be heading out."

Ellen, taking the cue from the disappointment on Sara's face, got up and cleared the table. "Come on, Tazzie, dinner."

Not wanting to miss the opportunity, and being stuck at home unless getting treatments, Sara blurted, "Ben, you don't have to leave. Unless you have an appointment early tomorrow, you can spend the night here."

"You have Ellen here and I don't want to impose."

"You could crash on the couch." Sara wanted to say more to convince him to stay. Aching to have additional time with him, to utter another word might risk too much. *Just stay calm. Don't push it. Give him space.* Waiting for his reply for what she was sure was going to be a declined invitation, she regretted asking.

Ben thought of the long drive back, how bone-weary he felt, and the lonely hotel room. Feeling welcome, not wanting to be alone, and appreciating the notion, "You know that's not a bad idea," he said, "if you have an extra toothbrush?"

Sara, barely believing her ears, felt like she had just beat Paula Radcliffe's marathon world record time.

CHAPTER SIXTEEN

Footsteps approached, sending spasms of erratic heartbeats pulsing blood through the tiny body's vessels. Even at that age, the baby sensed evil. Its small lungs moved fast like the wings of a hummingbird.

Low guttural growls and Tazzie's scratching at the door woke Sara. "Shhh," she muttered. Having only been asleep for a couple of hours, the clock on her nightstand read two-thirty. Still dazed, confused from the nightmare, lingering images were hazy. *Why are these happening? Am I stressed over Ben being here? What do these damn dreams mean?*

Not to be deterred, Taz continued clawing, leaving marks in the wood. "Tazzie, stop that!" Sara whispered.

Preventing Sara from getting back to sleep, the whimpering frenzy running in circles intensified. "Taz, no," she pushed the covers off. A twist of the doorknob and the dog bounded to the living room. She found Taz with Ben, who'd been up pacing. The second she saw him she had a bad gut reaction, the kind of sensation she got when she walked into an ER room and saw a patient in critical condition, the visceral sense she'd learned not to ignore. "Ben, what's wrong?"

Attempting to fight back nausea, he pursed his lips. After eating too much for dinner, his pancreas was rebelling. Feeling so ill, there was no way to keep it from Sara, "My stomach's bothering me."

"You nauseated?" She knew the look.

"Yeah, I'm sorry I woke you."

"I'll be right back." She went to the kitchen to get some ginger. Handing him the candied root, "Eat this."

He gave it a quizzical look.

"It's ginger. It works well for nausea. If that doesn't do the trick, I have a stash of marijuana muffins in the freezer."

Not wanting to put anything else in his bloated belly, he hesitated.

"Ben, we use it with pregnant moms." She watched him eyeballing the lump in his hand. "I've used it for my nausea from chemo."

Cautiously, he chewed it down and waited. Not caring if it was a placebo, Sara's presence or the ginger, he did feel better in a few minutes. "I think I can get some sleep now, thanks."

Sara sat atop the sleeping bag on the couch and patted it. "Come sit down with me." Her eyes rested on his face, eased of the painful contortions from moments earlier. She wanted to lead the way so he'd be comfortable communicating about his illness. "Even with the bandage on for my ribs, you can probably tell I've got breast cancer. I had a double mastectomy. It looked pretty bleak for me up till Zimmerman got me approved to be included in the research with a new drug." She went on to tell him a little about her history leading up to that day when they first met. Once finished, wishing he'd redirect the conversation back to himself, she sat silently. *I hope you can be open with me. It might help you.*

Despite what he just experienced, he didn't want to speak about himself. Rather than responding in kind, he shifted away from his discomfort. "How's it going with the study?"

"Remarkably well. They're talking of cure." Knowing he was holding back, like men tend to, sensing the resistance in the tight way he held his shoulders, she took a leap. "Want to tell me what's going on with you?"

Ben's larynx constricted. "What's to say?"

She let out the breath she was holding. "Anything you want to."

You're not making this easy. He felt her attention move into his body, loosening channels that needed to flow, sending a rush of heat flushing through him. "It's not good, Sara."

"Neither was mine. They'd given up on me. I'd given up on me."

Other than with his brother, Ben didn't share personal stuff. It made him very uncomfortable. He understood the value of getting things off one's chest, but with so much distrust living in his cells from bad memories, it was hard for him to let his guard down. He was moved by Sara's honesty, how humble she'd been with him. Torn about what to do, he opted to reciprocate to avoid hurting her feelings, not because he was highly motivated, and so he spoke. "I have advanced pancreatic cancer." He waited a long solemn moment. "You're a nurse, so you know what that means."

The ache in her chest was instant for although there was the high road, his being on a study and hers going so well, she was aware of the lethality of his disease. Determined to keep positive, she felt her heart missing beats when she said, "Well then, you're lucky Zimmerman has you on a trial drug." Taking hold of his hand, "You'll get better, just like me." Rampant thoughts spurted. *Before getting into my study this would have freaked me out, knowing he had no chance in hell. Shit, I had advanced breast cancer and I'm improving.* The rhythm of her heart slowed back to normal. "Ben, I really feel you can get

better. Zimmerman's one of the best. Just hold that idea."
Saying the words out loud replaced doubt; she believed
them herself.

Tazzie jumped up on the couch next to him.

"See, she knows. She found my cancer."

Ben patted Tazzie's head. "She's a great dog."

"She used to sniff my breast where the tumor was. I've
read of dogs finding cancers, diabetes, and alerting people
to seizures before they happen."

"I can tell you really love her, Sara."

The way he mentioned her name sent shivers down her
spine, similar to how she felt listening to Ravel's *Daphnis
et Chloe*. Devoured by attraction, she wanted to grab and
kiss him, drag him down the hall to her room. Were it not
for the restraint of her rib bandage she was sure she would
have seized the moment. "How'd you find out about
yours?"

The entreating softness of her countenance, their hands
enfolded, the way the light hit the contours of her body, and
the gentleness of her manner invited him to step into the
discomfort that blocked him from entering into a deep and
meaningful relationship. Much as he wanted to, he was
never able to totally conquer his timidity before now. With
the embers of chemistry starting to spark, he knew it was
time to unlock the door to intimacy and it had to begin with
opening up about his cancer.

While Sara listened, he told his story, about the
workup from his doctor for abdominal pain, the Stanford
Tumor Board, and his brother connecting him to
Zimmerman. Unexpectedly, the more he said the easier it
became. His nausea was all but gone.

"I know Zimmerman will take extra good care of you."
Consumed with wanting to slide over closer to him to allow

their legs to touch, she made her move and put a hand on his thigh. "You're lucky."

When the words were spoken, he was aroused from the motion of her fingers on his leg, and gently slipped an arm around her back. "I'm not hurting you, am I?"

Melting into him, "No," she absorbed the movement of his body as he leaned into her and their lips met. An affectionate several moments passed before she asked, "Want to come back to my room?"

They fell asleep holding hands, she wrapped up and in her nightgown, he fully clothed, with Tazzie on the floor.

CHAPTER SEVENTEEN

Ben woke up to the floral fragrance of Sara's hair, the rhythm of her barely audible breath close enough to feel on his cheek. He reflected back to the wee hours of the morning while the moon beat down on them, as word by word he unlocked the cargo of emotional baggage about his illness.

Watching her eyelids gently moving, she looked so defenseless with her arm slung to her chest and limbs showing the last tinges of yellow bruises from the intravenous lines. He yearned to take her in his arms to quell the need growing in his groin, a craving that surmounted other bodily sensations—the ones that scared him—the things he didn't want to talk about in the living room. Despite what he had held back, he felt comfortable with her and what that did to calm his insides was unanticipated. He wanted to reach for her, not just for sex but to connect with and protect her, to keep her safe, which surprised him. Whether it was changes in him from the illness, her accident and hospitalization, or the conversations they'd had, the closeness he felt with her gave him pause. He'd opened before and was burned. Not wanting to risk it, he couldn't help that she made him feel alive and he wanted more of it.

At a little past eight Sara's phone rang, waking her. Knowing who it was before answering, she smiled over to Ben and motioned for him to be quiet. "Mom."

Playfully, he put his hand under the sheet to find her thigh.

Sara's attention went to his touch while she gave an ear to Rosalie. "Yes, my friends are still here."

"For Christ's sake, when are you ever going to learn to take care of yourself!" The volume of her mother's voice increased. "I hope you got your sleep!"

Sara held the phone away so he could hear. "Yes, mom."

Ignoring what Sara said to her yesterday, Rosalie hounded, "We'll come out today then?" It was really not a question.

The heat of Ben's body did nothing to stop the chill that her mother's tone sent through her. Sara didn't want to lie again, and worse be caught in one, but her mother's indignant stubbornness left her no choice. "They're not leaving right away. Let me phone you after..."

Just then Ben sneezed.

"Who's that," asked Rosalie. "Where are you?"

"I'm home, mom. Where'd you think I was?"

Rosalie wasted no time in shrieking, "Are you with a man?"

From a sneeze? You can discern that from a sneeze? Hating that she lied and feeling cornered by her mother, she decided to come clean and suffer the consequences. "Yes." Ben's fingers moved gently on Sara's thigh.

"There's a man there with you!" Rosalie screeched, reducing Sara to a five-year-old, incapable of making a decision or demonstrating wise choices. "You told us not to come because you had a man coming to visit? Every stray in the neighborhood has to land at your place, Sara. When are you ever going to learn?" With that she hung up.

Sadly, she looked at Ben, who hadn't taken his sight off her.

"You okay?"

Wanting to move on, stuff and lock her reaction to Rosalie in a hidden mental box, Sara nodded. *Why does my damned mother always do this to me! I hate it!*

Seeing she was on the verge of tears, Ben said, "Talk to me."

Out it came. "She doesn't think for one minute I'm suffering? I'm struggling with cancer! She has to lay it on. There's no letting up with her."

Tazzie put her head up on the bed next to Sara.

Ben took his hand from under the cover and sat up. "How old is she?"

"In her seventies."

"Her generation didn't sit down and talk, like ours does." He understood this from dealing with his own dysfunctional parents. "Who knows what their cultural upbringing was or the habits they formed." He motioned to the dog, "We're all conditioned just like she is. Most women back when she was a child didn't have much of a voice. It was a very submissive era for them. She's probably making up for lost time now," he smiled, "and, being a little overprotective because she's frightened to have a daughter with cancer."

You don't know my mother. She has an edge, razor-sharp, that cuts. "I see what you're saying but still it's not easy. There's no way to reconcile with her. She knows how to push my buttons. This was nothing in comparison to some of the other.... I just have to work through it on my own, and I do."

"Trust me, I get it."

Feeling Ben's empathy softened the thorny pricks from her mother's words. The reverberation of the conversation evaporated into the reflection of light bouncing off his eyes, and all she wanted to do was cuddle up next to him and forget about the world of crappy relationships. "For a guy, you're pretty smart."

"Well, I won't dispute that."

"Figures," she laughed.

He stroked her face and while kissing it, "What's so funny?"

"I had a thought."

"What?"

Hearing Ellen stir in the adjacent guest room, "Shh."

"What," he repeated, "are you thinking?"

"You're pretty sensitive," continuing to laugh, "for an attorney."

"Ha-ha, very funny," he smiled and responded with a lawyer joke. "Okay smartass, what do you call a lawyer with an IQ of 50?"

"Hmm, let's see..." Looking puzzled, "I give up, what?"

"Senator."

The laughing and playfulness continued through Ellen getting dressed and leaving them a note, "Be back later, lovebirds. Stay out of trouble."

They got up and Ben showered. Aware she couldn't dress herself with only one available hand, he asked, "Would you like me to help you get dressed?"

The moment had arrived and she was unprepared. Feeling way too self-conscious, "No!" she stepped back from him. "I'll wait for Ellen."

"What if she's gone a long time? Don't you want to change out of those?"

Tears welling up, "I can't..."

Seeing the light drain from her eyes saddened him. "Sara, I want to see your body." His voice lowered, "Do you think I'm going to see something that will change how

I think about you?" He went closer to where she was standing. "Right now, all I care about is how I make you feel. I know how I feel."

"Yeah," she relaxed, "how's that?"

He reached toward her robe and opened it. "I want you. However you are." Leaning in closer, he kissed her and lightly made his way down her body, below the bandage holding her ribs, to her abdomen. He lifted her nightgown to kiss and lick her bellybutton, to caress her thighs.

When he brought his hand back up to her chest, she panicked and grabbed hold of it. "No, I can't."

"Come here," he guided her to the bed. "I want to be with you. Make love with you." Sliding his hand to her hip, he fondled her thigh and opened her legs. Ben kissed her neck, and moved down over the bandage, touching his lips to the area where her breasts once were. "You're so beautiful, Sara, inside and out."

Sara's muscles ridged into knotted tension and she pulled back. "Ben," she cried, "I can't do it."

"What are you afraid of?"

Reservoirs of emotions scrambled her mind, refusing him entry. It didn't matter that she ached for him, for normalcy, to realize her full sensual self. It was overridden by the fear she'd repulse him. "Ben, please, I'm not ready."

The more she resisted the more he wanted her. "Let me help you."

"I don't want your pity. I don't want any favors."

"That's what you think this is?" He put her hand on his swollen hardness. "I want you. Do you hear me? And I want to help you, for me."

"Ben," she sobbed, "I'm..."

"Tell me." His cheek rubbed her shoulder while his lips continued to find new areas. "Talk to me," he whispered in her ear.

"You won't want to be with me," she looked away, "if you see me."

Sitting up and taking her face in his hands, demanding attention, "Sara, I'm not going to hurt you." He held the gaze until he saw her eyes calm. "Have some faith in me."

It was like her first hot air balloon ride; she was frightened of heights and sure it would deflate and crash, yet once she stopped resisting she enjoyed herself. Without saying another word, she yielded. Feeling her acquiesce, Ben moved his hand over the bandage. The delicate motion of his fingers on places untouched by a man since her surgery brought memories clamoring to be liberated. Off came the first time she saw her scars and the pain she felt with the way the nurse looked at her. She released the torment she felt over her father's tears about seeing his daughter staring death in the face.

Finding his way to her panties, he gently pulled them down while his lips discovered places that sent her into waves of spine-tingling sensations. When she started to moan, he moved back up to carefully unwrap the bandage. Cautious to not press on her ribs, with his eyes on hers he unwound the last part. "Oh my, Sara."

Mistaking his sorrow for shock, for revulsion, and shrinking back in, *I knew it!* she tried to grab for the sheet to cover up.

Stopping her, "Don't," he took hold to remove it.

"I knew you'd…" she wanted to get up, leave the room and the shame where the bed was, the den of intimacy, to put it behind her. Unable to break away, his every kiss a magnet, drawing her in, deep inside to the festering wounds chaining her soul.

"Shh," he whispered into her neck. "All I see is you. All I want is you." Moving his mouth to her chest, he kissed every inch of her, "You're so beautiful," as his hands moved back down between her legs.

Every movement, every kiss, the feel of his warm skin on hers, released the tension from the last two years and the breakup with Henry. The balm of his touch soothed the soreness, calmed the ache, to help her slowly ease into a vulnerable acceptance of his passionate offering. Releasing thoughts, letting go any residual resistance, she disintegrated into a sensuality she'd never felt before. Aware of the union with him as he carefully maneuvered around her ribs, she disappeared into her body, alive only to the stimulation between her legs, the flush of heightened arousal, until she went out of her mind, over the edge into a frenzy of exalted rippling spasms. When nothing was left but ecstatic well-being, she broke into laughter. "Oh my God!"

They spent the rest of the day discovering ways to satisfy each other. The awkwardness she'd battled with, her scars, dissolved into their chemistry together, that inexplicable, magical connection that can only be physically experienced and not verbally or mentally described. More than orgasmic, the lovemaking between them was the beginning of the essential spiritual healing for both of them.

"Ben..."

"Uh huh?"

"Thank you," she whispered.

"Pleasure," he laughed. "How about an encore again tomorrow?"

Overjoyed with his proposal, "I would love to but," she remembered she had a treatment, "I have an appointment at UCLA that I can't miss."

"I'm staying in a hotel in walking distance. You could spend the night there with me and I'll bring you back Friday. Would that work for you?"

"You'd do that for me?"

"I'd do that for me," he laughed. "I'm scheduled to see Zimmerman on Friday anyway."

CHAPTER EIGHTEEN

They bid Ellen and Tazzie goodbye and headed out in Ben's car down the Pacific Coast Highway. Making the turn by Mugu Rock, "The Chumash Indians named that," Sara pointed to the promontory separating the sea from the road, opening ahead to a magnificent stretch of miles of visible coast.

"What's it mean?"

"Beach," she laughed.

"Leave it to the Indians to keep it simple. I didn't know they traveled down this far south. I thought they settled closer to Monterey."

"No, they traveled and traded from Monterey county to as far south as Malibu. So many of what they considered sacred sites are gone, destroyed by outsiders." Recalling the deep black hair and round tanned faces of the Navajo group she worked with, "It's sad that Indian tribes have been so decimated and what's left of them are beleaguered with problems: depression, alcoholism, lack of education, obesity, and all that goes along with those issues."

"How do you know about the Chumash?"

"Ojai. I was curious what it meant. I found out that the Chumash named it. I think it means valley of the moon, but don't quote me. I became curious to learn more."

"That's how you found out about your totem animal, the elephant?"

I can't believe you remembered that. "No, that was from a man, a student of one of the elders, who I met at the Navajo reservation where I did my clinical rotation while in graduate school. I don't know why it came up but one day he started to ask me questions."

"Like what?"

"Oh, let's see, what animal am I attracted to, what animal am I most drawn to at the zoo?"

Looking ahead, Ben saw a flock of seabirds in flight. "I don't like zoos."

"Me neither, unless they're saving endangered species or harboring wounded animals that need care. Anyway, I said 'elephants.' I always feel so sad when I see them in pens or performing somewhere. Breaks my heart." What she didn't say was she identified with those performing elephants, putting on shows in cages, needing man. "He went on to tell me about the importance of respect for nature, and that he sensed I had a strong connection with animals. He was right about that."

"So, he told you 'elephant?'"

"Yes," she laughed, "that's as good a guide as any."

"That's interesting because after you mentioned that to me yesterday, I remembered something I'd read about ancient elephants in America. Something about scientists affirming that mammoths and mastodons inhabited the Americas at one time."

"That's fascinating. Maybe their souls live on," she laughed. "Really who knows about these spiritual metaphysical things? Like when I'm thinking of someone and my phone rings, and it's that person. If anyone would be in touch with something like that, I think it would be the Indians. You can see it when they sense something."

"True," he smiled. "I respect the mysterious aspects of life. I admire Joseph Campbell's way of approaching it. He doesn't take it into an answer but stays with a questioning. There are a lot of things we can never know about, but we sure can be in touch with the awe."

Cruising along, they saw the whitecaps breaking on the aqua saline waters inviting surfers to remain afloat until sunset. Waves and ripples rolled in and out with a soothing grace, and Sara was tranquil as the saltwater air gave vitality to her lungs, now well healed.

She looked out over the deep mysterious blue expanse, feeling one with life. A few clouds moved across the horizon followed by seagulls dancing and diving to find their dinners. A large bottlenose dolphin jumped out of the water, succeeded by another and another, moving with the current. "Dolphins, Ben! Did you see them?"

"No, I missed it. Maybe there'll be more." His eyes were on the road. "You watch for both of us."

"Aww, what a sweet thing to say."

They arrived at the dinner destination she had chosen and Ben pulled in. "Very nice," he commented.

"Geoffrey's Malibu is one of the best. Every seat has a panoramic ocean view."

Situated where they could hear the waves, Ben took in the vision. "It's still working," referring to the marijuana he'd taken to curb the nausea that came in cycles throughout the day. "Your help and the fresh sea air. I have an appetite."

"I'm happy to hear that." Sara glanced around at others in the room. "It's funny, this place attracts politicians and famous people, yet the owner came up from the ranks of the working class."

"Lots of well-to-do did."

"Highfalutin' folk congregate here, so does the paparazzi, but for me," laughing, "want to know who I like best?"

"Who?"

"The busboys." She told him the story, the history of the place, that Jeff Peterson evolved from within the restaurant's company to become its owner in the late nineteen-nineties. "He started out as," continuing to laugh, she spat water, "a busboy."

And when the busboy came to refill their glasses, they told him what they were laughing about. "That gives me hope," he smiled.

Taking their time with the menu, they gave their orders to the waiter; both had soup made with wild mushrooms, which Sara said was good for the immune system. For the main course Ben ordered pan-seared Chilean sea bass made with heirloom tomato marmalade and basil oil. "Basil oil, haven't heard of that before," he said.

"Me neither," Sara smiled and proceeded to order herb-crusted salmon. Neither wanted wine. "Got to stay away from that while on chemo."

Noticing the vase of orange-red flowers on their table, "Zinnias," Ben felt the lance-shaped sandpaper texture of its leaf as he appreciated the lush succulent plants cascading down to the sand. "Lot of activity out there today," he said, referring to surfers riding the waves.

Sara, watching Ben appreciate the environment, felt satisfied and grateful to have this moment of perfection with him. *I could never have scripted this for myself, not in my wildest dreams.* "Oh look," she motioned to the server arriving with their plates.

Enjoying the meal, "You picked a winner," Ben took a bite.

"You can't beat the food and ambiance here." The rest of the meal was spent welcoming taste bud sensations, listening to the jazz being played in the background, and delighting in each other's presence. Content that they didn't feel compelled toward idle chatter, "It's so nice to be able to eat mindfully."

"Not sure what you mean," as he finished the last bite of his food.

"Paying attention to what I'm tasting, chewing my food. Not zoning out, like when I'm driving somewhere and arrive with no idea how I got there, distracted the entire time. I'm surprised I'm still alive," she laughed. "There are some things it's lovely to be present for. To experience the flavors of what I'm eating, the aroma, and not just related to food but what my eyes see, my ears hear."

"I guess the idea is to try to be awake for all of it. Easier said than done. My mind has a mind of its own."

"Whose doesn't?" Pleased to see he'd eaten everything, "How you doing?"

"No complaints. You," he motioned for the bill, "feeling better about that phone call with your mother?"

"I'd say you took good care of me, Ben." She moved her hand over to his side of the table, the warmth of his skin a sensual reminder of the beauty they'd shared. "My mom said I shouldn't pick up every stray that comes along."

"I take that as a compliment." He stroked her arm as they joked about dog metaphors.

"Thank you, Ben."

"For what?"

"Bringing up my mother." She lowered her voice, "I know I have to face it. I don't know what to tell her about us. My mother has a memory like a gorilla when it comes to me and," she took a sip of water, "I have to be careful or I'll never hear the end of it."

"Tell her we're together. That's all you need to say."

"You don't know my mother. She'll kill me with a guilt trip if I don't tell her what's up." *Me telling my mother I'm spending the night with you? Trust me, it's not going to be easy!*

The ride to his hotel through Malibu and onto Sunset Boulevard took them past the Lake Shrine Temple of the Self-Realization Fellowship. "That's one marvelous piece of property," she motioned ahead for Ben to see its sign. "Ever been there?"

"Don't know that I have."

"It's too late to stop now but another time—it's really beautiful. The Fellowship does good things, continuing the spiritual and humanitarian work of its founder, Paramahansa Yogananda."

"That's a mouthful."

"Yeah, sure is," she laughed. "I spent a lot of time here when I was into meditation. It has nicely landscaped grounds with a spring-fed lake full of ducks, swans, koi and turtles. Yogananda is revered as the father of yoga in the West."

"Didn't he come to America in the twenties?" Ben changed lanes to get beyond a driver going under the speed limit.

"Yes, I believe so." Sara closed her eyes and drifted off to before she married Henry, when she used to love to come and sit quietly, soaking up the peace she felt at the Lake Shrine Temple. She knew the Fellowship to be benevolent but couldn't stop the mental reminders of worshiping and beliefs, how they can tear apart relationships. Bad memories from her split with Henry lingered.

As far as she knew, Henry was still in the Descartes Global Movement, known as DGM in the closed circles of the elite, of which he was one. She had no problem with the original ideas and courses, to help people look at their thinking, at the very nature of thought, with the main premise being *thought is never the thing.* That she was fine with. However, when a group member graduated up to becoming "The Wise One," a vision attained through costly courses, and everyone else below them was deemed "The Unwise," that's where she drew the line. She argued this was judgmental, biased, elitist dogma. DGM labeled her *persona non grata* for disagreeing, and Henry was made to choose between the group and her. She was out and he stayed in.

"Cat got your tongue?"

"Nothing worth commenting on." She looked at the lights casting a glow to structures below and wished it were still daylight so she could see the mansions along Sunset. "We were so lucky with sundown tonight." They had stayed at the restaurant long enough to watch the sun transform into an array of red and pink as it brought down the crystal blue sky. "So breathtaking."

"Nothing compared to you."

"Oh, you're just saying that."

"Well yeah, I am. But let me tell you, the last twenty-four hours have been my best in months. Maybe years. Maybe ever," he laughed.

"Okay, now you're stretching it." A solemn wave washed over her. "You must have been with plenty of women." Clearing her throat, "You're sure you're not with anyone now?"

Taken by surprise, "No! Don't even think that. Do you actually believe I'd do that to you?"

"Ben, we hardly know each other. Our circumstance is so unusual and I…" She pulled back from telling him she felt she was falling for him.

"Sara, there's nothing unusual about how I feel, which I assume is how you feel. I'm happy with you."

Reflecting back to the images that had surfaced of Henry's goodbye and the bad taste it left, "I feel the same but I have my insecurities."

Not understanding her change in attitude made him uneasy. "Ask me anything you want." A car in the right lane coming too close for comfort caused Ben to swerve. Luckily no one was in the far-left lane. "What do you need to know to put your mind at ease?"

The effort Ben made took the edge off her worry. "Okay, that helped. Let's wait till we get back to your place though. I don't want to distract you while you're driving."

More thoughts bubbled up. Henry making love to her one minute and gone the next. An obese man entering a bedroom and a fussy baby flashed before her eyes. She wondered about there being a connection with the nightmares and a sense of betrayal she had felt most of her life. Henry breaking up with her validated this violated feeling. Her father being a workaholic and hardly ever home along with her mother's inability to show affection, to hold and hug her, reinforced issues she had with trust. Relationships with men, especially intimate and sexual, softened the unloved place in her heart. As long as she could make love, she felt loved. Now with so much stripped away, she knew that wasn't honest or real; it was a solution and a distraction. What she was opening to with Ben scared her. She needed to know that she could believe his word meant something, and that he wouldn't hurt her. She couldn't bear to open and risk that kind of pain.

CHAPTER NINETEEN

Back at his place, Sara turned on her cell phone and saw she had several messages from Rosalie. Disgust swelling under her skin, "My mother's in a tizzy," she gave Ben a look. Dealing with her was the last thing Sara wanted to contend with but she knew the longer she waited the worse it would get. Just the thought of Rosalie's reaction made her scalp tighten into what was sure to become a headache. *After such a great time with Ben, why this?*

First Sara got in touch with Ellen to see how Tazzie was and how much damage control might be needed. "Did you talk to her?"

"What do you think? How many times can one person ask, 'Is she home yet'?"

Pressure built in Sara's temples. "What did you tell her?"

"Not much. Just that you were with a very supportive friend who lived near UCLA, and who would take you for your treatment tomorrow."

"Oh no!"

"What? What'd I do wrong?"

"I'm here and didn't go to see them."

"I hadn't thought of that," Ellen's voice cracked. "I'm so sorry, Sara. I didn't know what to say. I forgot that your parents live close to UCLA. Your mother's going to have a hissy fit. Oh crap, Sara, I…"

"Oh crap, is right." Sara saw the puzzled look on Ben as he opened a window to let in fresh air. "I should have called her earlier."

"Why don't you tell her your cell went dead?"

"No, I don't want to keep lying. Plus, where can anyone go that there's not a telephone?"

"I feel bad."

"El, it's not your fault. I'm not mad at you."

"Okay, good luck."

Ben sat next to her, watching her stare at her closed phone, and waited for what she had to say.

"I just have to do it."

"It's really that bad?"

"It might be," Sara grabbed his hand. "I'll find out soon enough."

"Hang strong, kiddo."

Sara gazed around the hotel room at the upbeat lush furniture. Feeling the soft cushion of the latex bed beneath her and being in this lavish comfort, she wished she could just enjoy it with Ben and not have to confront the detour through hell with Rosalie. As sure as the clock would tick the next moment, for now the fun time with him would take a backseat. Sara heard the muffled laughs of people coming out of the theater across the street intermingled with the sound of ringing up her mother. *If only we were out there instead of...* "Mom, hi."

Urgency, beyond called for, "Where are you?" screeched through the line.

"I'm with a friend."

"I've been phoning all day."

"I know. I'm sorry. We've been on the road."

"Road? You have a cell phone, Sara!" Bitter sarcasm curdled in her outburst. "You with that man? Don't tell me you're with that man."

Sara wanted to spit out the sour taste. "Mom, please listen to me for a minute. I met him at Dr. Zimmerman's office. He's another cancer patient."

"What! You haven't got enough taking care of yourself you have to take this on?"

Ben, hearing the antagonism vibrate from the phone, drew a hand slash across his neck, indicating to get off if it was upsetting.

Sara motioned back a stop with hers. She was pissed off and roared, "Mother! I'm the one with cancer!" The dam had burst and what came forth was more than restrained communication; it was years of lacking what she'd needed and a plethora of hurt shoved down her throat. "I met Ben, yes, his name is Ben, and I care about him." Lowering her voice, "I'm happy with him. I haven't felt like this in years. It's good for my healing. It's what I need." Seeing Ben smiling and giving her a thumbs up, "I want your acceptance. But I'm a grown-up and if you can't support me, then maybe we should consider taking a breather."

"That would kill your father!"

Sure that her mother's carrying on and insensitivity to both of them was doing greater harm than anything she could ever dream of, and fed up with the manipulative histrionics, "You think yelling that now, at," she noticed the clock, "nine at night is going to help him?"

Rosalie went silent.

"Mom, I love you. And I love dad, but I have to live my life, whatever I have left. I don't know if the treatment will work. There are no guarantees with any of it and what I don't need is to have to deal with your accusations and anger every time we communicate."

Something Sara said got to her mother and the dramatics stopped. "You said that the treatment was working?"

Rare as it was, hearing the genuine distress from her mother was a relief. "I'm not out of the woods yet. I have another treatment tomorrow." Sara looked at Ben. "Would you like us to stop by after?"

"Both of you?"

"Yes, mom."

Ben nodded approval.

"I'll see you then." With that Rosalie hung up.

Sara rubbed her temples to release the tension, glad that it hadn't turned into a migraine. "Oh man," she gestured to her phone, "how can such a small little object bring so much intensity."

Thinking of his own family dynamics, he let out a nervous laugh. "Don't blame the phone."

"Throwing blame there is safe." Still pensive, "I'm glad that's over."

Ben wanted to get her attention off the conversation. "How about you lie down?"

"You in the mood?"

"Yes," he laughed, "but that's not what I had in mind right now." He went to sit at the end of the bed, took off her shoes, and started massaging her feet. "I'm glad it worked out okay with your mother."

"Me too. I hate that she's so difficult but I need her, Ben. I need a mom. Personally, I think everyone does."

"I know what you mean." He felt the texture of her soft sole rippling under his fingers.

The movement on her ankles was just right. "Ooh, that feels so good." Closing her eyes, "It hasn't always been easy for her. I don't know what I'd do if I had a son like..." She truncated saying, *Like crazy Jack.* As his fingers moved in circles, she drifted off. *A big fat man blundered*

down a long corridor, his mouth frothing as he made his
way to the baby.

"You don't like to talk about your brother, do you?"

"Huh?" Sara looked up at Ben. "I must have fallen asleep. What'd you say?"

"I asked about your brother."

"Actually, I don't know much about him." What was lurking below her awareness was the impact of a schizophrenic brother, a mother steeped in avoidance, and a father spending too much time away from home. When it was discovered that Jack was mentally ill, she was ostracized and humiliated by the kids in school. Her answer to being blackballed was to lose herself in sex. Promiscuity at sixteen cemented the memory block about her brother.

"Really?" Increasing the pressure on her left foot, she jerked back. "A sore spot?"

"Yeah, I'm probably holding onto a blob of stress." As he worked a circular motion with his thumb, she stopped flinching. "Not sure why, but I have trouble remembering things regarding Jack. I have a few fuzzy ideas of him being in the house. Nothing specific. One day he just disappeared. From time to time, he pops back in at my parents' unannounced. It used to be more frequent. Dad thinks it's because he's on his medications." A stricture of sorrow welled up in her chest. "I think it's 'cause they don't like him. My mom's ashamed she has a crazy son. My dad can't handle it."

"Any idea where he is now?"

"Last thing we heard about him was a phone call that he was found in Colorado on a park bench by two police officers who brought him to an emergency room. He was admitted to a medical ward to get his diabetes and hypertension under control and then he was transferred to the psych ward."

"How'd you find out about that?"

"Jack has my parents' phone number in his wallet as an emergency contact. The psychologist on his case phoned them."

Seeing tears oozing from her closed eyelids, Ben asked, "Something you wanted to say?"

"I worry about the impact Jack has on my father's health. I'm sure his heartache over how he turned out played into his heart attacks."

Concerned about adding more stress to the equation, "Do you think it's wise to bring me around to meet your parents? It might be too much for your father."

"I think it will be okay. He'll see I'm happy. Can't be sure of anything with Rosalie, but my dad's a good guy." She wiggled her toes, "That was a great massage," and opened her eyes to a troubled expression on Ben's face, and for the first time noticed the traces of yellow on his skin. "That's enough talk about my family."

"You are looking better now," he admitted.

"Thanks to you. But seriously, Ben, I just want to be with you. Whatever happens with my parents will work itself out. I hope you feel the same."

"Sara," he leaned in to kiss her. "Does that answer work for you?"

"I'm not sure. You'll have to try it again," she laughed. As his tongue parted her lips promising what was to come, she ran a hand down his back, and around to his hardness, drinking in the freshness of his flesh—lines of muscles formed and flat in all the right places—moving in delicate rhythm with hers. They took their time riding over the edge to satisfaction.

"That was lovely," she purred.

"Um-hum."

Snuggling into her, the pulsing of his hand on her thigh vibrated aliveness. Raising it to her mouth, she moved her lips over the soft creases on his palm and kissed his fingers. A while passed before finally asking him, "How come you've never been married?"

"Mostly I just never found the right one. And circumstances…" Ben explained that he was with someone, a model ten years younger. They were together for over four years when she cheated on him. He found out piece by piece, like in a bad movie, "with receipts for men's clothing items that weren't for me, a theater ticket I hadn't gone to see with her, nor had her friends." On confronting her, she told him she'd stayed with him for security but the passion had long gone out of the relationship.

"That's awful. How long ago was that?"

"Long enough. What about you? You've been married. What happened?"

She gave him the short version of life and betrayal with Henry. "Appears we both have trust issues. Ben…"

"Yes, I'm here," he laughed.

"Do you feel safe with me? I mean do you trust me?"

"You're adorable."

She nudged him with her right elbow. "Come on. Answer the question."

His underarm perspiration increased. "You know men don't like these kinds of conversations."

Knowing they had a lot to lose by not facing their insecurities, being honest and upfront with each other, "Ben, this is important. This is what was bothering me earlier in the car ride. It's not easy for me to feel secure."

"Trust isn't something you can just talk about, Sara."

"What do you mean?"

"It takes time to develop. We're in a honeymoon phase and due to our circumstances might never leave it, which would work for me. I hope that's the case." He didn't want to continue; it felt too heavy, serious.

Sensing there was more, "What? Tell me."

"I just don't know how either of us will feel about anything tomorrow. That's what my ex taught me. But it's not just from that. I see how people are. I'm jaded about trusting in something forever. I can't help it." There was more, much more, but not now. Maybe never. He hated even thinking about the abuse from his father and the impact it had on how he felt about relationships.

"Do you think we might be able to learn to trust each other; to find out if it's safe to be authentic and open up?"

"It's an interesting idea but how do you make that happen? I don't see any way. No easy switch to flip on and there you are."

"I think I do."

"How?"

"We honor our word, don't say something just to create an effect in the other, be honest but sensitive, and stay open to conversation. How's that sound?"

"It's a tall order," he smiled.

"Come on!" She whacked his arm.

"Enough talking. Come here." He drew her in with a kiss that moved down her body.

"Answer the question," she cooed.

"Let's just see how things go," as his lips and tongue found places that sent her into another dimension.

CHAPTER TWENTY

That night Sara slept fitfully as haunting images whirled around her psyche of the fat terrible monster and the frantic baby. *He removed the blanket and grabbed hold of the baby's kicking leg. The big man's distorted face kept changing like a kaleidoscope until it morphed into someone who looked familiar.* Sara moaned and turned into Ben, feeling the smooth texture of his skin on hers as she drifted off. When they awoke, the nightmare was forgotten.

Later that day, while Sara was getting treatment, Ben phoned his brother and brought him up to speed.

"You're sure about this?" asked Michael.

"Yes, she's different than anyone I've been with. It feels right."

Hearing the cheerfulness in Ben's voice, "Well, you do sound good. Can't fault that."

"Thanks, Mike."

Sara and Ben made their way through Beverly Hills on Wilshire Boulevard, where the Beverly Wilshire Hotel is located. The site was strewn with memories for Sara. She and her girlfriends hung out there, shopping, eating, and walking around people-watching. So did her brother Jack.

She was just a teenager out with a couple of friends when she ran into him walking alone with a Cuban cigar in his mouth, ranting a boisterous sermon.

"Look at that fat guy talking to himself," Sara's friend Mattie said loudly enough for him to hear.

Agitated and uncertain of what to do, Sara ignored him as he approached.

Janis, the other girl with her, shrieked, "You can smell him from here."

Sara's throat seized when he looked right at her, and she prayed he wouldn't say anything.

Pointing the cigar towards Sara's face, "Well, look who's here," he gave a slow once over to the other two. "And who are these sexy ones?"

Heart pounding, Sara took hold of Mattie, "Let's go!"

Jack latched onto Janis' sweater, pulling her to him. "Take your hands off me!" she struggled to get free.

His eyes went vacant as he babbled unintelligible sounds into thin air. "Did you hear that?" He grabbed hold of her butt. "She wants me."

Janis broke loose and yelling at the top of her lungs, "Help!" She instantly drew a crowd.

Jack was taken to the Beverly Hills police department and held for sexual battery of a minor. The charges were later dropped when it was determined he was schizophrenic, and had not been taking his medicine. He was then readmitted to the mental facility he'd been in and out of since Sara was a baby. On finding out he was Sara's older brother, the girls' families forbade them from associating with her. Sara was bullied and shunned as rumors spread through their junior high school, and for weeks she came home in fits of hysterical crying. It threw her into a depression. Rosalie was driven further into herself, incapable of showing any affection. Sara's attempts to hug her mother were met with, "For Christ's sake, leave me alone." Irving drowned himself in work until years later he had a heart attack, but by then the family was broken.

With Ben, Sara's heart was opening and raw emotions threatened to detonate at the slightest provocation, ungluing this incident and others hidden by amnesia.

As they continued down Wilshire Boulevard on their way to her parents, Sara was reminded of that earlier time with Jack. *Why is this coming up now?* Resisting the repulsion of the shame and embarrassment made her feel sick to her stomach. The image from the last nightmare surfaced and she remembered the fat man's face. *It was Jack's! Am I that baby? Oh my God!* Just as sure as her intuition spoke, so did the doubt. *No, it can't be. Stop plaguing me! Damn it!*

The longer she remained quiet, the madder she became. *Why now! Leave me alone!* She wanted to light a match and burn the image of Jack out of her mind. *What do you want from me! Go away!* By the time they passed the Beverly Wilshire Hotel, the tension in the car was palpable.

"What's wrong?" asked Ben. When Sara didn't respond, he pulled over on to a side street. "We don't have to go there." He turned the ignition off and waited.

Feeling Ben's attention on her, confused images from her dreams surfaced and she didn't know what to do. *What's going on? Why is Jack coming up now? Did you do something to me, Jack?* Trying to push it out of her mind was of no use.

Stay quiet. It'll pass. She'd learned from her mother that being high maintenance was repelling. *I hate the shit my mother spews around and I sure as hell am not going to dump this on Ben. I won't put him through that. I won't risk worsening his condition. Who the hell wants to be around that crap anyway? Breathe.* She calmed enough to barely utter, "No, it's okay. Let's go."

"Sara, it's obviously not okay. Talk to me."

"I can't." The young girl inside her was afraid once again of losing what mattered. No longer was her crazy brother a topic of impersonal conversation, something her parents had to deal with—now it was visceral. *I don't want to lose you, Ben.*

Waiting for her to look up, "You were the one who said we could learn to trust each other if we open up and communicate." Seeing the anguish on her face pained him. "Okay, here's my answer. I'm ready. Talk."

"I know you're right, but…" she stopped herself.

"It wasn't easy for me to open to you at your place about my cancer. But when I did, I felt better." He reached a hand over to her. "Talk to me."

He's right. The weight of the memories pressing in on her broke loose. "When I was diagnosed with cancer I started to have nightmares."

Ben watched her words steam up the windshield and condense into beads of water.

"I'm still trying to make sense out of the impressions. Honestly, I'm not sure what's just a bad dream and what actually happened, but I think my brother came into my room," she wept.

Ben's hand on her leg, he felt the heat in her body intensifying. "Go on."

"I'm so ashamed to say this."

"Get it out, honey."

Turning her cheek away, her focus on the hazy outline of a tree outside of the car, she continued, "The same scene repeated, over and over. There's a baby in a crying frenzy. A man comes into the room and pulls the covers off—he touches the baby's private parts." Like in her nightmares, the blur from the foggy window lent an uncertainty to what she saw. Running her hand across its cooling, moist glass surface, the image of her dream faded.

"For the longest time the face was a stranger, a freak. Then it changed into my brother's. And I wondered if I was the baby and Jack did something to me." Sara's body shook. "At first it only happened in sleep, then flashes came to me in the daytime." She wiped the moisture off her hand onto her sweater. "Just a few minutes ago as we passed the Beverly Wilshire Hotel, I remembered something that happened." She told him about the incident that had been triggered.

Listening to her meek tone speaking those horribly difficult words, Ben saw red. "Oh my God, Sara, no one should ever have to go through that! What a bastard!"

Guilt from the conjecture, and that she'd spoken it out loud, insinuating that Jack had molested her, gripped her. "I shouldn't have said anything about the dreams. It was wrong of me."

"It wasn't wrong of you. You obviously needed to get it off your chest."

"How do I know I'm not associating an imagined fat and scary person with him just because Jack's overweight? I just can't be sure anything actually happened."

"It did that time with your friends!"

"Yes," she whispered, "even so, he's ill."

Ben didn't realize that what she told him had stirred up his own issues; for one, the unresolved anger he had over his relationship with his father. "So what...Jesus!" Choking back his exasperation, he clutched the steering wheel. "This doesn't piss you off?"

Drained, she slumped back in the seat. "Honestly, I don't know what's inside me, Ben. I'm not sure what's real." She repeated, "I shouldn't have said..."

"You still want to go to your parents?"

The disgusted edge in his delivery made her stomach quiver. "Yes." She sat silently for several more minutes, looking around to regain her composure. Cars drove by, a red light changed to green, people crossed the street, and she was ready to move on. Noticing that Ben was still watching her and hadn't shown signs of retreating or rejecting her, she said, "I'll be okay, let's go."

Clenching the wheel so tightly, that it could cut off circulation to his fingers, Ben started the engine and continued driving. *What kind of assholes live in this world?* By the time they made their way to an early thirties Mediterranean home on a palm-lined road, Ben had calmed down. He looked at Sara and said, "You sure?"

"Yes."

Before they made it to the front door, it opened and an older couple stood side by side, she with dyed-blond hair bouffant style, and he balding in front with strands of comb-over. Well-preserved, good-looking, short and slim for their ages, the man smiled and the woman frowned. Rosalie's hands were on her hips, shoulders held back, and Sara knew the mood her mother was in the minute she saw her.

"How's my girl?" Irving stepped out to greet them.

"Dad." They hugged and he met Ben with a handshake.

Staying put, Rosalie snarled, "We've been waiting over an hour. What happened to you?"

Sara, followed by her father and Ben, walked the brief distance to her mother's corrosive glare. The beam Rosalie shot coiled Sara's stomach. *I can see our last phone conversation didn't sink in.*

"You've been crying." Rosalie swiped a rough hand across Sara's cheek. "Go clean yourself up."

Ben wanted to grab Sara and turn around until he saw Irving motion for Rosalie to leave it alone.

Sara, wanting to jump down her mother's throat, instead ignored the gesture. "Mom, this is Ben."

"Mrs. Phillips," he held out a hand, which she grazed with hers.

"Come sit down and eat."

Sara went to the bathroom to freshen up. One look in the mirror, seeing the eyeliner smeared down her cheeks, *What a mess!* A few splashes of water on her face and she was ready to brave the meal.

CHAPTER TWENTY-ONE

The inside of the Phillips' place instantly made Ben feel welcome. It had a calm inviting ambiance that oddly relaxed some of the edge from the bitter attitude Rosalie had generated outside. Still on guard, he mulled over the paradox of the harmonious environment Sara's mother created in contrast to her cold personality. *This is a surprise.* He wondered if Rosalie provided an aesthetic home to balance her mental turmoil while Sara was growing up, and speculated if this had played into Sara's easygoing demeanor and the facile way she worked through her issues.

Ben eyed the spacious kitchen that adjoined an open dining room with Spanish Mission red terracotta tiles, giving a cozy appearance. The table had comfortable bamboo chairs and was set with multicolored plates. Adorning the walls were original Matisse and Kahlo paintings in vivid colors, giving Ben the distinct impression that somewhere in this family there was money. "Nice." He admired the two women in the Matisse, their bodies disproportionate to their heads. "It goes great with the room."

Sara looked at the Matisse. Studying the black circles around the women's breasts, she felt a soft flow of energy that had been moving into her body since making love with Ben. "I like the portraits he did after he left Paris and moved to the French Riviera."

"How come?"

"They're more laid-back and revealing, compared with his earlier work."

Giving her a knowing look, his hand brushed against her backside. "Well, that makes sense."

A blush came over her cheeks. "My aunt Beth gave these paintings to my mom."

Rosalie brought Hawaiian chicken and rice with green beans to the table and flashed Sara a look that told her to keep her mouth shut. The artwork came from her sister, the one she was self-conscious about, the lesbian Beth, with a wealthy girlfriend. When Beth's partner died, sending her into a tailspin, Sara's mother was the only one in the family to visit her. Upset with everyone else, Beth changed her will, giving everything she'd inherited to Rosalie; along with the art, the small fortune that afforded the Phillips the purchase of their house.

Glaring at her daughter, "Sit down and put some food on your plate," she contorted into a mass of aged wrinkles. Her full-red grotesque lips, taut from anger, set in her ghostly powdered face sent a chill through Ben's bones. As they sat, flailing a finger at Sara's bandaged ribs, Rosalie hissed, "When does that come off your arm so you can drive?"

Cringing on seeing her mother's ready-to-attack dilated pupils, "My ribs," Sara corrected her.

"Ribs, arms," Rosalie shook her head. Motioning to Ben, "Go ahead and start eating. Don't let it get cold." Eyeing Sara, daggers sprang from her dark brown eyes. "When?"

"I can remove the bandage any time. It's just to control the pain, not for the fracture."

Ben's blood boiled as he flashbacked to the hostility his father flung around, the discomfort he grew up in, and was pissed with the crap Sara's mother was slinging at her. After all he'd just listened to on the car ride over, once more he wanted to grab Sara and get the hell out of there. *Why's your father just sitting there and doing nothing?* It was similar to his own mother's condoning behavior, enabling Ben's father to destroy their family.

Rosalie, a pressure cooker ready to burst, stuck a fork into a piece of chicken. "So when?"

Ben shifted uncomfortably, while Irving ate.

"Probably a couple of days, Mom."

Nodding satisfaction, Rosalie put the food in her mouth. "Eat. You're too thin."

Irving looked over to Ben, his face soft with relief. With this Ben understood that diplomatic silence was his effort to avoid an escalation.

Sara, following her father's example, ate without saying another word.

"So Ben," Rosalie took a mouthful of rice, "Sara tells us she met you at Dr. Zimmerman's office?"

Shoulders tensed, Ben sat up straight. "Yes, that's right."

"Do you care to tell us?" Rosalie coldly prodded.

Seeing Ben's face go stiff, his neck flush stress, Sara swallowed the vegetables she was chewing. "Mom, I don't think this is the right time."

"Let the man speak for himself!" Rosalie slammed back.

What a bitch! Ben, digging his foot into the tile floor, knew he had to step cautiously and give the woman what she wanted. The message was clear; this was Rosalie's lair. "It's okay," he spoke slowly, modulating his tone to hide his reaction. "I have cancer also, Mrs. Phillips. I went to see Dr. Zimmerman for a second opinion."

"Who's your regular physician?"

"I was being seen up in Palo Alto by a Stanford team."

Rosalie's ears perked up at the mention of Stanford, a prestigious private university for the rich. "They have good doctors there." Making eye contact, "Why'd you need to come all the way down here?"

Sensing that he might be getting somewhere with her, Ben settled back into his chair. "My brother roomed with him in medical school and told me he's involved in some studies that are unique only to him. Zimmerman is touted as the best. He's the cavalier that heralds the new and untried in oncology research."

"That's some language you use, Ben," she laughed, breaking the tension in the room. "And your brother is a doctor?"

Sara's next bite of food went down easier, now that Ben had managed to lay the first stone with her mother. *Way to go, Ben!*

Hearing a lilt go into her words as she leaned in closer, Ben saw Rosalie was impressed. "Yes, he's a surgeon." He'd broken the ice and decided to squeeze it for what it's worth. "On faculty at Stanford."

Wanting to applaud his aplomb and hug him, Sara knew Ben had found her mother's Achilles heel—status, the loftier the better, was winning points for him. "Ben went to Stanford also. So did his parents."

Ignoring Sara, "You a physician, Ben?"

"No, Mrs. Phillips, I'm a lawyer. I work at NASA."

Sara suppressed a laugh.

The rest of the meal continued uneventfully. They spent it in light banter with Ben catering to Rosalie's lead about movies, celebrities, charitable events, and mahjong. When it was time for them to leave, Rosalie turned to Ben. "How long will you be down here?"

"Maybe two months. But I'm not sure."

Poking Sara's right arm, "Bring him again."

On the ride back Ben broke the silence. "I don't think your father said two words the whole night."

"He's no dummy. Once you put it out there you never know what's going to happen, and worse, you can never take it back."

"Good point." He watched the red taillights of the car in front gain distance as it picked up speed. A police van with flashing lights came out of the blue and pulled it over.

"Not smart to speed in Beverly Hills." Seeing the driver slow, "They'll ticket you for going a mile over the limit."

"Palo Alto is the same." He thought back to the conversation with Rosalie. "Your mother is some piece of work. How do you put up with it?"

"I don't know," she cracked the window. "What choice do I have?"

Hearing the resigned exhaustion in her voice, "Have you tried to have a sit-down talk with her?"

"Too many times to remember." She shifted her position to get more comfortable. "You saw how she communicates. You heard me try last night. How long did that last? The minute we arrived over there tonight her attitude was back, heavy as ever."

Annoyed with Rosalie's audacity, Ben said, "She's got a mean streak in her. How could that stress not be making you come apart at the seams?" Intent on the road, "I doubt I'd put up with it."

"It's complicated, Ben. I want to have a different relationship with her. I've wanted that all my life." Feeling a draft, she rolled the window back up and noticed the lit storefronts featuring costly displays—the abundance of stuff that people use to substitute for what they lack inside.

"I've thought of walking away from trying to get through to her, from her caustic remarks, how she puts me down, but it pains me more to think of having nothing to do with her. Then there's my father to consider. He's tried to get us together through the years, before his heart attacks. After that, we just settled into learning how to be with each other." A black dog in the back seat of a car passing by, ears waggling in the wind, made her smile. "It's not all bad."

"Really?"

"We used to go out for lunch every once in a while. Find neutral things to talk about?"

"Like what?"

"Her charity work, shopping, movies—mindless things."

"It doesn't get to you?"

"It gets to me, all right. But how many tears can someone cry over what isn't going to change? It's how she is. I don't know—you get used to it, and then just occupy yourself with other things. It's been hard to avoid her since I got ill."

"Families!"

"Huh?"

"Oh nothing." He looked at the white icicle lights on trees, as he swung into the parking area where he was staying.

"The stores are still open." He got out and walked around to help Sara. "Want to go for a walk? Get some fresh air?" *Get our attention off family bullshit!*

"That sounds nice. We can both use some extroversion after that meal," she laughed.

"I'm glad to see you can laugh about it."

"It's a stress reaction. None of it is funny—but enough of that for now." What she didn't say was what being with him, their intimacy, was doing to help her transition through these flare-ups with Rosalie.

Taking their time, they came to Jerry's Famous Deli on Weyburn Avenue. "I used to go there a lot when it was a Hamburger Hamlet," said Sara, gazing in the window at people eating. "Best hamburgers in Los Angeles. This one and Sunset were my favorite hang-out places."

"I was at the one on Sunset years ago." Noticing her flinch, "You okay?"

"Yes."

Turning to face her, his forehead wrinkled. "You sure?"

"I have a high threshold for pain and don't want to let it stop me," she winced again.

"Seriously, if you need to go back…"

"My ribs are sore. Sure, every once in a while they hurt. Going back to the room isn't going to change that." Moving in closer, she felt the heat of his body. "Plus, there's probably less activity outside than in the bedroom with you."

He planted a kiss on her lips. "Sara…"

"Yes."

"I never anticipated meeting anyone like you."

Thinking back to their lovemaking, and how considerate he was, taking his time to find positions that wouldn't hurt, thrilled her. "I hope the intense feelings we're having aren't just because we're ill. Do you think that's what's happening with us?"

Without hesitation, "I'm sure that plays a part but even if we weren't…no," he shook his head, reaffirming his words. "There's so much about you, the way you look and talk, the little things you do, and how you are with your mother with all she dishes out. You cope so well with the hand you've been dealt. And that smile of yours is a killer."

"I think I need another kiss."

Continuing on, hand in hand, they walked past the Westwood Village Theater where she'd seen movies and stood in queues outside for premieres. They rounded back up toward UCLA and turned right on Le Conte Avenue to stop and admire the Geffen Playhouse.

"That's a nice looking building."

"One of my favorites. Lot of memories here." She went on to explain, "It's one of the first structures in Westwood Village that was built in the late nineteen-twenties and restored in the seventies, including the beautiful courtyard with a tile fountain." Appreciating the architecture, "This place is a class act. Come on, let's have a look." She grabbed his hand and walked him up to the glass front doors to have a peek inside.

"Very nice brick work. And I like the tile roof."

"Me too. Last play I saw here was Steve Martin's *Picasso at the Lapin Agile*. Ever see that?"

"I didn't know Steve Martin wrote a play."

"Oh yes, he's a genius playwright. I think he's written several. This one was incredible." Motioning for him to sit next to her on a brick tree planter, "There are two protagonists, Picasso and Einstein."

"That's a combo." Watching her so animated, eyes sparkling, reminiscing about a good time made his body feel lighter.

"Yes, and they're in a bar, the Lapin Agile in Paris. It's hilarious. The whole play is one long conversation. Einstein is on the verge of the theory of relativity and he gets into this dialogue with Pablo Picasso about talent and intelligence. All sorts of other characters who interact with them walk in and out with agendas they're communicating from. There's this one guy who has prostate problems and won't listen to anything unless it's about sex or booze. You have to see it. I laughed myself silly. Saw it several times."

"That good?"

"Oh yeah."

"I've always liked Steve Martin." He playfully traced her cute upturned nose. "Just never had him figured for an intellectual. Has it ever been made into a movie?"

"I don't know." She crinkled her face where it tickled from his touch. "Don't think so."

"Check it out and we can rent it."

Sara loved the idea of renting a movie and cuddling up with him. "Oh, that'd be so great, Ben. We could make popcorn, snuggle up."

They returned to the room a little after ten. "That walk felt so good," she kissed his arm. "I feel really blessed."

"Blessed? With all you've been through?" What he didn't say was *and that shit with your mother*.

"But I'm okay now. Someone must be watching over me. They got that embolism resolved. I haven't had any problems with the blood thinner, and I think I can probably get this bandage off in a few days." Pressing her leg against his, "Trust me, I am lucky, and pretty soon you'll get luckier."

"You've an infectiously great attitude. I love that about you."

She ignited. "You said the L word."

"Very funny."

"Are you," she snickered, "taking it back?"

"I'm not."

"Not what?"

A breath away, "Not taking it back," he smothered her in kisses, maneuvering around her bandages, as they made their way to bed.

CHAPTER TWENTY-TWO

Ben woke up a little after daybreak, drenched. Sara was fast asleep next to him. Unlike times in the past from a bad dream or fever, this was different. His answer to doctors questioning him about night sweats since the cancer diagnosis was always, "No, I haven't had any."

Sara's peaceful face, angelic to his eyes, didn't stop the heartache that he had turned a corner, not the one he'd hoped for. The synchronous rise of her chest in unity with his—life—was a gift he didn't want to throw away by dwelling in the anguish that there might not be nights of movies, popcorn, and cuddling. That would serve no purpose other than to rob him of whatever precious time he had left, and as long as he lived, who knew what turn the next corner would take him to. Being keenly aware of his senses and keeping his attention on what was actually occurring gratified him. That alone was miracle enough. As his thoughts shifted from horrible outcomes back to the bed, to Sara, the ache in his heart drifted to the ethers. He let his pajama bottoms dry without waking her.

A couple of hours later, "Good morning," Sara nestled into his chest. "How'd you sleep?"

"Not bad," he lied.

They had just enough time to eat and get to Zimmerman's office by eleven for Ben's appointment. As they made their way, listening to the hum of the wheels on asphalt, a piece of gravel flew up hitting the windshield and chipping the glass. "Oh no," Sara put a finger on it to see if it went through. "It's smooth on the inside. Maybe you won't need to fix it."

His stomach turning sour, he glanced at the tiny crack that was still intact. "It'll need to be taken care of so it doesn't spread."

"If you'd like, we can try to contact someone when you bring me home."

"It'll be okay till I can get around to it."

Sara looked over at him. "You're sweating. Are you sure you're okay?"

"Yes." Swiping a hand across his brow, he knew his squeamish gut was making him perspire.

"You don't look okay. Are you sure you're fine to drive?"

"Yes," he swallowed down the saliva accumulating in his mouth. "It's warm today. I don't particularly do well in this heat."

Catching the glare of the sun on the bumper in front of them, "It's been hotter than average and is expected to continue for another week." With a distinct tone of suspicion in her voice that Ben noticed, Sara said, "Well, I'm glad we're on our way to see Zimmerman."

Zimmerman entered holding a syringe, "It's nice to see you two together." Looking at the needle, "I'm short a nurse today so let me go ahead and give you this." Moving closer to Ben, shadows of yellow on his sclera became more apparent. "How you doing?" He swabbed him with alcohol, injected the liquid, and disposed of the needle.

"Okay."

"No abdominal pain? Nausea? Vomiting? Difficulty moving your bowels? Blood in your stool? Night sweats?" Zimmerman rambled off at a rapid pace as if it was one long question specific to pancreatic cancer.

Knowing it wouldn't change anything were he to answer truthfully, he shook his head. *Let her think what she wants to, what she needs to, for as long as I can I want to make her happy.* "Nah, I'm okay. Sara's been taking good care of me." And he did feel better in the air-conditioned room.

Relieved with hearing what she needed to, Sara's stiff shoulders eased.

Nodding approval to Ben, Zimmerman caught sight of Sara releasing her taut grip on the handle of the chair. "How's Michael?" He shifted his line of questions into small talk. "I haven't communicated with him in a few weeks? Candace okay? And what's their daughter's name?"

"They're doing great. Melanie."

"Right, she's in college now? How are your parents, Ben?"

"She's at Berkeley. Haven't been in much contact with my folks lately."

Ben was aware that Zimmerman knew from rooming with Michael that their dad drank, and when he was intoxicated he became belligerent. The boys avoided him, but their mom, having no escape, took to the bottle and became reclusive.

Not expecting to hear Ben say he was out of touch with his parents piqued Sara's curiosity. Driving up Highway 33 back to Ojai in silence, it weighed on her that there were things about him she didn't know. Surprises and what they brought—disappointment and life changes—the holding back disturbed her. She had hoped that when he invited her to open up, he'd do the same. Now she feared it might be one-sided.

Ben broke the silence as they passed through Mira Monte, on the outskirts of Ojai. "I have an idea," he slowed for a red light. "Neither of us has an appointment till next Tuesday when I have to get another shot. How about we head out of town and spend a couple nights at the beach somewhere? I think the ocean air would do us both good."

"And Tazzie? Ellen has to work and I've already been away from her for…"

"Bring her. We'll find a dog-friendly place up the coast."

Sara's concern moments before turned to anticipation, and when they arrived, Ellen commented, "You look radiant."

"Ben worked his magic on Rosalie. You're not going to believe it." She filled Ellen in on what happened, that they'd be heading out, and asked, "Where's my girl?"

"Out back."

The dog wagged ferociously, threatening to break in half as she smothered Sara with licks. "Hey my girl, we're going on a vacation." When Sara was at her worst, Taz was by her side in an abiding loyalty. Tazzie was always there, saying, *I'm here for you for as long as these legs and body will carry me.* Her heart was opening to Ben, but excluding Tazzie was out of the question. She was grateful he was willing to include the dog in their plans.

While Ellen helped Sara get ready, Ben searched the net for dog-friendly hotels. The Sea Gypsy Motel in Pismo Beach had plenty of rooms with ocean front accommodations; he made reservations on his credit card. "We're all set. I think you and Tazzie will like the spot I booked." He pointed to a suitcase. "Want me to take that to the car?"

"What about you? You don't have any clothes with you."

"I have an overnight kit in the trunk. A habit just in case and," he motioned to his feet, "these will be fine at the beach," referring to his Teva sandals with rubber soles. "I can pick up some shorts and a t-shirt on the road. There's shopping from here to there, isn't there?"

"This is too damn good to be true." Grinning like a Cheshire cat, Ellen answered, "There's great shopping in Santa Barbara."

Looking in the mirror on the wall in the bedroom, "Too expensive," Sara brushed her hair.

"I don't mind. Something convenient to get to and we'll be good to go."

"You're so easy going, Ben." Ellen smiled at Sara and gave her a look that indicated she was thinking more than she was saying.

"What?" asked Sara.

"Nothing, it's nothing," laughed Ellen.

"Come on," prodded Sara.

"I was just thinking about the way you look at each other. It's obvious you two have a special connection."

Sara blushed.

"Okay, enough from me," said Ellen. "Have a great time, guys. I'll hold down the fort."

"You going to stay here while we're gone? You don't have to." Sara petted Tazzie. "No furry friend to feed, and you're working."

"I'm here. Too lazy to pack up, shop for food, my fridge is empty." Ellen giggled, "Yours is full." Walking them to the door, she joked, "I'll bill you for my gas to work."

At a Gap store in Santa Barbara, Ben purchased a couple of pairs of khaki Bermuda shorts and t-shirts. From Lazy Acres market, they left with two bags of organic food.

As they pulled up to the motel, the fresh salt air sent Taz circling and whining to be let out. Ben checked in, unpacked the car, and helped them into the room, where Sara put away the food. "That was so nice of you to get a studio with a kitchen."

"Hey, we don't have to leave the room. Eat, watch the ocean, and make love."

Sliding glass doors opened to a comfortable patio overlooking the smooth rolling motion of the water. Sitting out on the deck, soaking in the remaining late afternoon sun, Sara took in the expanse of sand and pebbles that led to waves breaking into froth. Listening to the sea's splashing rhythm and the melody of children playing, "I'm so happy."

"*So* happy." He emphasized so. "How do you define and measure happiness?"

"Good question. I don't know that you can quantify it and how can a word ever touch on something so elusive and subjective?" A hodgepodge of thoughts came forth. "Objects are easier to label than emotions." She heard the words coming out of her mouth, and saw some of her old conditioning arising—a carryover from the ideas of the Descartes movement—concerning thought and its lack of application when it merely points to a thing and is just a representation. "I just ran a bunch of mental jumble in my head and have come to the conclusion that none of it is important, except," she got up and leaned over him, her lips on his, "this," she laughed. "Call it what you want, measure it how you can, who cares—all I know is I never want this feeling to end."

Absorbing the warmth from her kiss, the rhetorical question dissolved. Now he wasn't bothered about what tomorrow might bring or what had transpired before. The only thing that mattered to him was that he was exactly where he wanted to be, sitting beside a woman he knew he could not improve on. *I could live like this, moment to moment, and take what comes without trying to control it.* He relaxed into the realization that he was okay, no matter his fate. It filled him with a deep sense of connectedness with life that calmed the lingering nausea in his belly. Ben gave Sara a knowing smile.

"Twenty-five cents for your thoughts."

"You've updated that idiom to include inflation," he laughed.

Their laughter and chatting continued as the sun drifted below the horizon's curvature into the mysterious space that separates earth from sky.

CHAPTER TWENTY-THREE

Waking to the fresh ocean air and sounds of the tide coming in, Sara beside him and Taz at their feet gave Ben a sense of belonging. It was how he imagined it should feel with family, unlike the hyper-alert style from the unpredictable environment he'd grown up in that made him feel abandoned and inadequate. Years of wanting approval from his father, striving to do his best in school, Boy Scouts, doing chores around the house were received with silence or resentment that he didn't live up to his dad's standards. One kind word, one mention of support, a simple *That's my boy* would have meant the world to Ben but instead he heard, "It's not good enough," and "You're not good enough!" Worse than the critical words were the fits of anger sounded in drunken rage. He never understood why his father took to the bottle; it'd happened a couple of years after he married Ben's mother, before the boys were born.

The unmet love he'd held inside wanted to reach out and find fulfillment, but it had been dashed too many times in the past, leaving him reticent to open—until Sara. Something about being with her was different, and safe. What the source of the heightened emotion was—whether it was the cancer, a view of death never this macroscopic before, or that he was unabashedly falling for her—didn't matter. With Sara he knew he was home, what he'd yearned for all his life.

A flow of air from Sara's parted lips grazed his cheeks, returning him to the sensual presence of their bodies. Embracing the tranquility of Sara in repose, *You gave me renewed purpose, meaning to my very existence that I had*

*lost with the futility expressed by the Stanford Tumor
Board, and I want to make you happy for the rest of our
time together.*

Once dressed, Ben was out on the patio with Tazzie, while
Sara prepared coffee and breakfast, when something caught
the dog's attention and she took off like the wind.
"Tazzie!" Fumbling to catch her, Ben's foot caught in a
pocket of sand, throwing him off balance. He hit the ground
calling, "Tazzie!"

Hearing the commotion, Sara panicked and ran as fast
as her aching body would carry her after her dog chasing a
small poodle headed for the highway. "Tazzie," her voice
cracked, "come back here!" A searing pain throbbed in her
ribs as her legs barely kept pace, until Taz stopped.
Grabbing the collar, she dragged her to the room, "No! Not
okay!" The bang of the slamming glass door sent Tazzie
cowering off to hide in the bathroom. "What got into you?"
She tightened the ace wrap around her ribs to lessen the
burning sensation, wishing it would also hold in the
pressure building inside her.

Ben came in, unhurt, and apologized.

"Not your fault. She's never done that before." Still red
in the face, trying to catch her breath, "I don't know what
I'd do if anything ever happened to her."

"She's okay now." Assessing where his knees had hit
the grit, he wiped away some loose granules and sat down.
"It's over. The other dog's okay."

The disabling tsunami of anger turned to grief. A
magnet of fear, envisioning the worst-case scenario brought
forth tears that Sara could no longer contain.

"What's going on?" Ben puzzled.

Like descending a mountain on skis, picking up speed, she could not stop the eruption blasting out of her. "I don't know what I'd do," she gasped, "if I lost her."

Ben motioned to the chair next to his. "Sara, come here."

Slumping down beside him, the heavens opened and out it poured, *it* being a story about a traumatic incident she'd had as a teenager in middle school after her brother's arrest, after the hoopla eventually fizzled out. She had made a new friend, a boy named Greg, who'd invited her to a party where some popular kids would be. But that night Sara overheard the laughter and the mumbled, "Crazy house." The kids were making fun of her. On that dark, cold night she'd run home alone and refused to go to school for a week. To assuage the pain his daughter was going through, her father adopted a golden cocker spaniel from the Humane Society. The dog became her constant companion, her salvation. She had not been without one since. Dog after dog, loss upon loss, their lives too short-lived, deeply mourned, they were her children. She hated the goodbyes—they were never easy.

"I just remembered I had nightmares for weeks of people gossiping that I was crazy. I'd wake up with no comfort except for Lucky." Sara's sobbing eased. "For years she was my only friend."

"Your dog's name was Lucky?"

"Yes, she was so cute, Ben. I think the first time I can really recollect being happy was with Lucky."

"That's why you named her that?"

"Actually, she came with the name and we kept it."

He reached a hand to her smiling lips. "You feel better?"

"Yes." She wiped her cheeks. "Thanks."

"Thanks? What'd I do?"

"For letting me vent. Not many times in my life I've been able to do that. And I'm usually uncomfortable opening up."

"What about Ellen?"

"Yes, of course, although that's different."

"How so?"

"She's a woman." Sara laughed. "But I don't always have her when I'm in a funk, and by the time she's off work or we do connect, it's passed."

"You do move through things well."

"Yeah," her bloodshot eyes brightened. "One thing I've learned is if I wait long enough everything changes."

Ben noticed her focus shift inward. "Something else?"

"I don't know," she wavered.

"Go ahead, tell me."

"The consequence of pouting and crying is that it only makes things worse. Ultimately, what good does it do? It took some learning and hard lessons for me to see that what I do that negatively impacts others also ends up hurting me. Besides, I think it's my basic personality to let things go. My dad's like that. I'm fortunate in that respect." She became introspective. "My mother, on the other hand, can't let go of her bitterness. Maybe seeing it in her has been an antidote for me. I don't want to be like that."

Tazzie, back at his side, prompted Ben to say, "If only we could trust and forgive like dogs."

Sara rubbed the spot behind Tazzie's ears that set her paw tapping. "It's their nature. For them it's easy." Reflecting on the mean girls in school, "With a rare few exceptions, like Ellen, I'm more comfortable with men than women, but still talking about sensitive things has never been easy, even with them."

Massaging her neck, "Probably 'cause they hurt you the most," he felt the tautness loosen from her muscles. "You seem okay with me."

"It's different with you. You don't judge me. And what you've already helped me through..." At a loss for words, she smiled, "I can't explain it."

"You don't need to." From the initial moment they'd made love when she exposed her vulnerability with him, to the outpouring since, something in him had been enticed to feel deeper than he'd ever gone before. The intimacy they shared invited trust. That she'd been through so much yet didn't carry around a lot of baggage gave him confidence that displaying his vulnerabilities might not end badly. He knew what he wanted to do. What he needed to do. Ben waited a few minutes to be sure she didn't have more she wanted to say. "There's something I want to talk to you about." It was something he'd been thinking about all morning.

The seriousness in his tone scared her. *Oh shit! What have I done? This outburst over Taz and in the car the other day. I should have shut it down!* "I'm sorry. I couldn't help..." She was apprehensive that she had turned him away. *Why the hell did I let that out? I'm such an idiot!*

He comprehended where she was heading. "Don't worry about that. I'm glad you got it out."

"Oh, good," she exhaled relief. "Then what'd you want to say?"

Looking into her eyes, he took hold of her hand. "I want to marry you."

What! Her skin felt loose as she sank into a whirlwind of thoughts. *Why?* She was caught completely off guard when Ben was so matter-of-fact—no romance, no "I love you," no leading up to it, just a flat-out statement, not even a question. Not that it would have mattered, the button was pushed. *Marriage!* Her parents weren't happy, she couldn't get away from the bad energy she grew up in fast enough, and her own previous attempt at nuptials had ended in misery. Statistics spoke that all is not well that begins in holy matrimony. Since she first saw Ben, there was no hesitation that she wanted to be with him, the only resistance her own insecurity that the attraction that possessed her wouldn't be reciprocated. Now with this sprung on her, still in mild shock, "What!" She nearly fell off the chair. "You're kidding?"

"No, I'm serious." Without getting into much detail he told her, "I've been thinking of my family, how distant my parents are from each other." Breaking eye contact, "It's just not a good scene. But never mind that. I've always wanted my own family. Never felt part of one until spending time with you."

Oh no! The only other word beside *marriage* that got her hackles up was *family!* Both were allergens she could do without. Still too engrossed with her own internal dilemma of how to get off the subject and return to the bliss of falling-in-love-without-legal-commitment, she paid no mind to questioning what he meant about his upbringing. Wanting to soften the blow, "That's so endearing, but we don't have to get married. I'm not running away from you." Feeling as though her brain was turning to paste, she feared they would lose the incredible happiness they shared.

When Tazzie licked Ben's foot, he kidded, "Taz is saying yes for you."

"She knows you're a good guy, Ben. So do I. But come on, why are you bringing up marriage?" She shifted in the chair. "We hardly know each other and what we do know is our situation is unusual."

"Do you love me?"

Sara hesitated. It wasn't a question of loving him but where the answer would lead.

Ben pulled back and became quiet. Her reluctance to respond was misunderstood.

Sara's heart sank, *What the blazes am I doing?* Conflicted, all she could think of was Henry and the discomfort of the failure of the first try. She vowed then, never again. *Shit! Things change when you get married. It's the kiss of death!*

As his face grew darker, there was something in his hunched-over expression that got to her. Nothing was left to do but be honest and pick up the pieces, no matter where they fell. "Ben, I didn't have good luck with marriage my first time. I just don't see why…"

Relieved once he understood her hesitancy, "Maybe you should listen to my reasoning. Hear me out." Taking a minute to formulate what he wanted to say, "I've worked hard all my life, own my own home and car, have savings in the bank, and a retirement plan with NASA. I don't want to leave any of it to my parents, and my brother doesn't need it. I want it to be put to good use and know you'll do that."

On hearing the get-my-affairs-in-order comment, her stomach rose to her throat. She regretted letting her mind run rampant without any attempt to understand. "Don't talk like that. You're in the study. I don't need you to do that for me. How about we just let things be and see what happens?"

"Sara, I don't know how long I have."

"Nobody does."

"Sara, I want to do this for you. I need to do this for myself. What you've done for me," he stopped to gain composure, "has changed everything. Since getting my diagnosis, I've thought of little else other than my having cancer. Then you came along, and I'm not living under this big black hopeless cloud anymore. You did that." He paused, looking deep into her eyes. "In the brief time we've been together, you've taught me what it is to trust and this is my heart saying thank you, I want to share my life with you, and I love you. I love you, Sara."

"What about Tazzie?" she joked to release the resistance that she had not yet worked through.

"Of course, Tazzie. I know you're a package deal. But joking aside for a minute, I'm serious about this."

Sara stared out the door to the ocean beyond, the ebbing and flowing, whooshing sounds of waves crashing on the shore, and people walking on the beach. Watching the curl and color of the water change and break into ribbons of rainbows on the wet sand, "How about," she said, "I heat up that coffee that's turned cold? After we have it, let's go for a walk. We're not going to do any marrying this weekend, which will give me time to think about what you've said."

CHAPTER TWENTY-FOUR

Ben and Sara, with Tazzie in tow taking her time to sniff every possible thing she could, made it a slow stroll along the beach. Glad that the discussion about marriage was shelved, Sara had time to let her head clear enough to listen to her heart.

The creek entered the ocean and sand dunes stretched into a row of eucalyptus trees. "Wow, so many butterflies." Tugging on her leash, Tazzie nosedived into a group of succulent plants. "Doggie perfume," laughed Sara.

"There must be hundreds of them." Ben's eyes followed a huge golden-winged monarch gliding with ease. "It's pretty romantic here." He kissed Sara's neck.

"Hmm," she groaned, "keep it up and we'll need to head back to the room." It felt good to be in his arms, have his lips press on her skin, melt into fluidity with him in motions that brought pleasure. *It's never been like this before and I don't want it to end.* Echoing comparisons with earlier relationships, Sara thought of the years she had learned to fill herself up with attention from men. Driven by an obsession not to experience the pain of her mother's rejection, she'd lost herself in sexual liaisons, one after the other, until her marriage to Henry. When he left, she fell in and out of one meaningless fling after another. Up till intimacy with Ben, sex was a substitute for abandonment— her mother emotionally, and her father physically by drowning himself in work. *Being with Ben is so different.* Another flash of murky image rose before her, *a fat hand on a baby, a sickening touch, inching upward. The man's face was a blur.* Moving through like a storm cloud, it was gone.

Ben, lifting his lips from Sara's neck, "The doggie perfume got to me."

"Very cute, Ben." She handed the leash to him, "Here, you take her."

Pointing to the pier, Ben said, "Let's check it out." At the very end where waves rolled by the pilings and sea otters played, he watched the boats cruise by. "It's perfect weather for boating."

"Sure is."

Tazzie circled, indicating she needed to do her stuff.

"Ben, would you mind taking her? I'll catch up with you in a few minutes. It was a lot of commotion this morning and I'm a little sore."

Lingering at the waterfront, she watched him walk away and it hit her, *Why am I waffling? We both have cancer, for God's sake! What if... No, don't go there.* She couldn't keep the thoughts from daylight. *What if he doesn't make it? What if I don't?* Sick inside, torn over what to do, she needed the space to look at why she was so resistant to his proposal. *I'm stuck! Shit!* A while passed preoccupied by the angst of indecision, the tenuousness of having cancer, and dreading it could all slip away.

The noise from a kid rollerblading caught her attention. She watched his swift movement in and out of people walking along the pier, gliding with ease, allowing nothing to stop his forward motion. Observing him, she saw something about herself that surprised her. *I always give to others what they want but am I really giving what's important?* A flashback of crying when she was a baby sent a frost through her, and she wondered, *Is there a connection with the dreams and my resistance to completely giving myself to a man?*

Now, open and raw, she knew it was Ben's love that gave her what mattered. *He's accepted me unconditionally, my wounds inside and out. Everything about me, as is. He gave me what I needed more than anything else, what no one's ever been able to do.* Awe moved through her, pulsing into her cells. *He helped me to find myself and to be okay to just be me.* Feeling his attention on her, she turned to see Ben with Taz at the other end of the quay. Doubt about marriage resurfaced but with a lot less sting. *Do I make this leap of faith?*

Ben was at a grassy area waiting for Tazzie when he looked back down the long pier to catch a glimpse of Sara standing alone. He knew she'd stayed there to get her wits about her, to sort out in her mind what she wanted to do. That also gave him time to look at his own motives. *I want to do it for you* played in his head. *It's important to me. I don't want my money to go to waste, my entire life*, and then he saw yes, he wanted to do it for her, but what he really needed and had craved was to belong. *I need to be important enough to you. Is what we have sacred enough that you'll commit to me in marriage? Will you claim me, Sara? Will you? While we still have time?*

Strolling up Pomeroy Street while window-shopping, they came to a funky hippie jazz house that served lattes and cappuccinos. Situated outside were a few circular arts and crafts painted tables reminiscent of the sixties. "My favorite kind of place." Noticing a bowl for dogs to drink from, "Tazzie, water," Sara commanded.

Taz slurped as Sara perused the menu written in chalk on a board outside the entrance. Pointing inside, beyond a small stage with set of drums, "Look, Ben," she motioned to paintings on the wall with a sign indicating they were from local artists. "Reminds me of Ojai."

The delight she expressed over the simplest things was infectious. Appreciating the positive effect she continued to have on him, *You're very easy to please. So spontaneous.*

"I want a latte."

"You want more caffeine?"

"Decaf. But right now I don't ever want to go to sleep. Don't want to miss a thing." She broke out in an Aerosmith's song. "I could stay awake just to hear you breathing, watch you smile while you are sleeping, while you're far away and dreaming." Drawing a crowd brought her to an end.

Clapping, cheering, and "Don't stop" erupted.

"Take a bow," laughed Ben.

In good form, she curtsied, as Tazzie tried to grab her own attention.

"Okay, you sang for it. I'll get you that decaf latte," he smiled. "And one for me."

"Really? You want another cup of coffee?"

Relieved that he wasn't plagued with the nausea that had increased in the last couple of days, "I think I'll be okay, and if not," he lowered his voice, "there's always the pot."

While Ben was ordering, Sara reflected on his marriage proposal. Surprisingly calm inside, an intuitive place spoke to her. Henry was history and she didn't want her mother's bitterness or the nightmares she'd had to hold her hostage from another committed relationship. Realizing that *things are never what you think they'll be* brought the crystal-clear awareness that the problem wasn't with marrying Ben, but rather the trauma living inside her. With him or not, married or maintaining the status quo, the bad past experiences could surface at any time and reactivate. She saw that the mind doesn't differentiate what's long gone from the reality of the present, and that triggered incidents seem as if they are happening now. It was then she understood that her pondering, with its limitations and blocks, could never comprehend what her heart already knew. *What we have comes once in a lifetime.*

Tiny insignificant lingering doubts about commitment, the voices of ghosts haunting and asphyxiating, were all but gone as Sara looked through the door to see Ben in the line to purchase coffee. She watched him inch forward, the way his legs carried him confidently, how relaxed he was, and the comfortable ease in which he held his hands. It was these hands, his touch on her scarred chest, his believing in the trust they were developing, how he made love to her in and out of bed, clothed and naked, that taught her that sex doesn't equate with real love. The kind she'd always dreamed of—intimate satisfaction, feeling whole, and the complete giving of oneself—was what she had with Ben. For the first time in her life, Sara knew what it was like to be loved, and to love in return. Coming from a grounded place, her decision was made.

Footsteps on cement, the aroma coming from the café, a smooth fresh breeze from the sea, and a mountain of other microscopic sensory happenings sang to her as Ben approached with two steaming cups. Inhaling the latte, "Oh, that smells so good." She watched him drink his and pointed at the mustache of milk across his upper lip. "You look like one of those commercials."

"Think I should grow a real one?"

"Nope." She spooned froth from her drink. "Ben."

"Uh-huh."

"Yes." With flushed cheeks and eyes aglow, her huge exquisite smile repeated, "Yes."

"Yes, I should grow one?"

"No."

"Then, yes what?"

A sip of latte and, "I will marry you."

Jokingly, he replied, "What, the latte did the trick?" Inside, he felt like a warm day after a long hard winter when snow begins to melt and birds take to exhilarated flight. Her "yes" filled him with an awesome overwhelming joy, like the sensations of hearing Sibelius' *The Swan of Tuonela*. Had he not experienced it first-hand, the magic they were together, he would never have believed it possible.

"That and a couple other things," she laughed. "Seriously, I'm very happy about it. And since Palo Alto is not too far, why not head up there and I can meet your folks?"

Overshadowing what he'd experienced just moments earlier, the question pierced him. As long as he was away from his parents, particularly his dad, and kept his focus on other things, he was okay. "No." The mere idea of interjecting them into what he had with Sara sent repulsion through him. "No!"

Sara was surprised by his shift. "Want to talk about it?"

Ben's torso tightened. "Some things just aren't worth talking about."

She waited for him to say something.

After a long pause, staring blankly into space, he turned back to face her, "It's not a good idea."

Seeing a deep sorrow in his eyes, the sadness he kept well hidden, "Want to tell me why?"

Knowing it was not healthy, yet afraid of getting lost in all the stress kept at bay, he remained quiet. He had never opened up about it to anyone; it was nothing he even contemplated. Now with Sara, he felt differently. They sat there for a long time and finished their drinks without saying another word, until he broke the silence. "Let's go for a walk down to the beach." Once away from crowded places, he disclosed, "They are serious alcoholics. My father is very abusive."

"Oh, Ben," she sighed.

Introspectively, he continued, "I grew up with shouting, swearing, denigrating, slapping, belt beatings and poundings by him." A cold tremor ran through Ben's body. "He'd come at me with his bulging, bloodshot rheumy eyes, and burst tiny red vessels around his cheeks, from too much sauce."

"Ben, you're shaking," she moved closer to him. "I had no idea."

His heart sped up as his vision became blurry. "There were so many evenings he'd go missing. My mother was frantic with worry. We'd get phone calls in the middle of the night to come get him from the local bar." He told her of the embarrassment of having a father who was labeled a lush and a worthless drunk by his peers, his Stanford buddies. Word got around to Ben from his friends. "That humiliation was far worse than the physical beatings." It was the scarring he carried around, from a father who never showed love or respect and was socially shameful. "Mom couldn't stand up to him and became a boozer as well. She never leaves the house."

Heartsick from hearing that, "I'm so sorry." She felt for him, but couldn't help asking, "Wouldn't it hurt them to not know?"

He tightened his hand into a ball of hatred. "No!"

The abruptness jolted her. "Ben, listen to me, please. We don't know why he is the way he is. Alcoholism is so complicated." Wanting to make some sense for him, "Just a visit, perhaps even closure. If you don't make the effort, you may live to regret it."

"That's the whole point, Sara. I'm not going to live." Wanting to hit something, to strike out to relieve his frustration, he pounded the sand. "The fucking stress with my father probably predisposed me to this damn cancer!"

Anguished over seeing him so distressed with his face twitching from the pressure, she appealed to him. "Maybe it would help you to face him with it."

He hated she had to listen to this crap about his family, and saw she was struggling to get him to consider a visit. "Sara, I can't."

Stroking Tazzie's head, she stayed still.

Just then he was distracted by a flock of seagulls floating across the sky in harmonious formation, circling around the water's edge. A couple of them landed. One sounded a cry and drummed its tail while the other one moved its aside. "Look Sara, they're mating."

She reached for his hand without comment.

Aware of her touch, he slowly drew back to his compassion for Sara, helping to calm his anger, lending another perspective. *Maybe she's right. Maybe it would help to talk to my father. But I don't see that happening. How many times can I try and keep getting nowhere? All the drunken rages. No one to get through to. It's like talking to a corpse.* He felt the pulse from Sara's wrist beating against his arm. "If it means that much to you. You've certainly shown me what's possible. We could drive up and see Michael and Candace. They should be home then. They're usually off on weekends." His gut turned flips at the thought of seeing his parents. "And we can stop by my folks and head back on Monday."

Knowing this was not easy for him, "We could even head out early Tuesday morning if you schedule Zimmerman for later in the afternoon. I'm sure he'd do that for you, for us," she smiled. "Just tell him it's our wedding present," was her attempt to lighten things.

A cool breeze picked up. It was time to leave.

CHAPTER TWENTY-FIVE

Asleep with a smile on her lips, Sara dreamed of a man. *A bewitching mirage, his blue eyes radiating, cast a spell that echoed a forever love.* She knew in her invisible protoplasm, the nucleus of her existence, she'd always loved him and the idea of him before his personification came to be. He, her heart's desire, was her safe sanctuary.

Then, peaceful rest was interrupted, and the movie screen froze. She tossed and turned as the subconscious images reeled onto her subliminal screen. *Lying in bed, the baby heard the footsteps pounding on the wooden hallway floor outside the bedroom. She clenched her tiny legs together as the door slowly creaked open. A mere shadow appeared first, the face indiscernible. A heavy odor loomed over her small body. A night lamp by her crib cast a dim light, enough for the murky black mask to crumble away piece by piece, until with clarity she saw—Jack!*

Snuffling from her dog woke her. Watching Taz jerk and grunt, fragments of Sara's dreaming were still present as she visualized the mental portraits of two men. The first held the same eyes sleeping next to her. With pieces of the puzzle sliding into place, removing doubt, she knew that the other one was her brother. Seeing the overlapping of then and now, she unclasped her legs, releasing the burden she had been viscerally bound by. Turning to look at Ben, it felt as if a hundred pounds of fresh air entered her lungs, cleaning out the remnant debris of the blockages that had prevented her from experiencing a vulnerable, intimate relationship before him.

Having fallen asleep thinking of what he told her about his family, she wondered if Ben's purging stimulated her nightmare. *I can't help feeling there's more to learn. But what?* Ambivalence consumed Sara. *I need to see what happened if I'm going to fully heal.* Although her body felt lighter, her mind was burdened. *There must have been a lot of psychological trauma inflicted on me as a baby. Jack, what did you do to me? What am I missing? Something doesn't make sense.*

Ben turned over, wrapping his arm around her hip, and the abhorrence she felt towards her brother was absorbed in the benediction of her communion with him. New courage sounded that she was ready to confront her demons. *Your love is giving me the strength.* Determined not to put this on him with everything he had to contend with, she kept her dream and realizations to herself. *I'll tell you when the timing is right.* They got up and had breakfast in the room.

"That's nice of your brother to let us stay with him," she reflected on the conversation Ben had had with Michael the previous night. "He sounds so supportive of our plans."

"Yeah, he's happy for us. So is Candace. They're good people. You'll like each other."

"I hope so."

He watched her push her plate away. "You all set?"

"Yes," she looked around the room at what they needed to pack.

"I'm glad we're getting an early start to avoid the heavy traffic."

"Gorgeous." Sara looked at the shoreline of coastal beauty. Sparkling jewels of sand mesmerizing her, she said, "I'm glad we're not going to go through Steinbeck's salad bowl inland." The smell of seaweed and humid air filled her lungs. She felt encouraged that she was handling the trip better than expected, and was happy she'd started to gain some weight. It was the reassurance needed that she was heading into a remission. *I hope you are also, Ben.* Smiling, *I'm holding onto the affirmation that we're healing together.*

"Steinbeck's one of my favorites." A maroon Jaguar sped past in the left lane, going well over eighty. "What's the hurry, buddy?" Watching it disappear around a bend of mountain, "Crazy drivers on cell phones, texting."

Having seen way too many auto accident casualties in the emergency room, she wanted to change the topic. "Which of Steinbeck's books do you like the most?"

"I read *Grapes of Wrath* last, for what must have been the tenth time. I loved *Of Mice and Men*, but I have to give it to the grapes. What a great story. The ending when Tom Joad is on the run and makes the speech that he's going to tirelessly advocate for the oppressed are some of the best lines in contemporary literature."

"Yes, that was terrific."

"When I was in law school, I used it to build a case in moot court."

"Did you win?"

"No," he laughed, "it wasn't a good legal defense for tax evasion." He could hear his father's criticism, *You didn't do it right!*

"That's funny." She caught a glimpse of a surfer riding a crest of rolling water.

On the back seat, Tazzie's snout pointed upward as they crossed Morro Creek, surrounded by marshy sage scrub and various shades of green chaparral. Proceeding north to Cayucos, the road turned into a winding two-lane route. "This doesn't bother you, does it?"

"No."

"Lot of people don't like these curvy stretches but the view is spectacular." Taking in the scenery before him lessened the twinges of resentment toward his father.

Gazing ahead, Sara hummed the Aerosmith song she sang earlier.

"Want to turn on the radio?" He enjoyed music, especially classical and jazz, but was not in the mood for any, preferring a quiet drive.

"Not really, you?"

"I'm fine. You have a good voice," he said with his focus glued to the narrow strip of road.

"When I was young I used to stand in front of my parents' bedroom mirror and sing, pretending to be a Broadway star."

"Ever seen a show there?"

"No, but I'd love to."

Knowing he would never see New York again, he kept his thoughts to himself. *I don't want to hurt you, Sara. You've had enough of that in your life.*

"Ben, you okay?"

"Oh yeah, sorry. I got distracted."

"Anything you care to talk about?"

"Nothing worth mentioning."

With the winding road behind them, they continued along the straight stretch of seaside highway to Cambria by rocky cliffs and beaches strewn with people under umbrellas. Sara caught sight of a man playing ball with a dog. "Look, Tazzie!"

Yelping, Taz jumped up to the rear window to keep the sandy-haired pooch in view as long as possible.

Seeing a sign that Hearst Castle was nine miles north of where they were, she said, "Can you imagine partying there?"

"I would have preferred to have been a fly on the wall. Drinking and cavorting just isn't my thing. But," he laughed, "on the other hand, if it were just you and me invited up for a nice quiet weekend, that I could do."

"The opulence boggles the mind. Living on a 40,000-acre ranch, with a zoo no less? Hearst was a piece of work."

"What do you mean?"

"His political career. The hemp controversy—he wanted to make it illegal so his forests would become more valuable. His pool is lined in gold. When is it enough? Not to mention his very public affair with Marion Davis while still married to his wife."

"Millicent Veronica Wilson," added Ben.

"That's her name?"

"Yes. She was another interesting character."

"How so?"

"Her mother ran a Tammany-connected and well-shielded house of ill repute near the base of political power in New York."

"You're joking!" Her mind went off in scandalous funny images that threw her into fits of laughter. She took a swig of water.

"I wasn't kidding," he smiled over to her. "How do you think Hearst felt about his mother-in-law running a whorehouse?"

She burst into paroxysms of glee. "Stop making me laugh."

"That sound coming out of you reminds me of the time I saw a kookaburra."

"A what?"

"It makes a sound like a hyena," he laughed.

Unable to gain composure, she spat what she was drinking. "What is it?"

"You like to spit water when you laugh," he joked.

She looked around for something to wipe herself with.

"Tissues are in the compartment on the door. Let me know when you're finished with the liquid and I'll continue."

"Oh stop." She patted the moisture off her face and lap. "What's a kookoo…"

"Kookaburra. It's a bird native to Australia. I saw them when I was there." Prodding her to more laughter, "They're sexually…" he glanced over at her.

"Sexually what?" She still couldn't stop laughing.

"Dimorphic."

"What's that?"

"It means there's a difference between the male and female," he chuckled. "A very important thing nowadays."

"Oh, come on."

"No, actually, I read that they do have different sizes and rump colors. The female is larger."

It took Sara a few minutes to calm down, "You saw them in Australia? When were you there?"

"After graduating from college. I went with some friends. It's a great place." Seeing the speedometer approaching seventy-five, he slowed down. "I was hiking with another guy and heard this laughing. It's really amazing."

"Sounds fascinating. I've never heard of them."

"You probably have but didn't know it. Even though they're only in a relatively small part of the world, their laugh is used in soundtracks for jungle movies."

"So that's a kookaburra?"

"You got it," he reached over to pat her leg.

"Where else have you traveled?"

"Just about everywhere. I worked part-time jobs during college and spent it on travel with friends. You?"

"Outside of several places in the U.S., I've been through Europe, some parts of Africa, Mexico, and Canada. I'm interested in different cultures, lands, seeing new things. It doesn't have to be fancy, just how people live. The smiles on the people in Africa, their sparkling big eyes despite the poverty, that's something I'll never forget." In reflection she continued, "We take so much for granted here." Looking to her side mirror to see Tazzie sniffing the wind, "So many are without shelter, food and water, when there's enough wealth in the world to help everyone have these fundamental needs met. I just don't get why people have to suffer like that."

The speed now registering sixty-five, he hit cruise control. "As long as we humans have our egos, there will be suffering."

"True," she looked back at Taz. "Tazzie's enjoying the ride. I wonder what she's smelling out there."

"Talk about getting needs met, probably a McDonald's inland somewhere," he laughed.

"Don't get me started again. My ribs are definitely improving. I took a lot of abuse from you with all that laughter. That was great."

Smiling over to her with one eye on the road, "I give good laugh."

"Stop it!"

Before they knew it, they were driving by Carmel among white sand beaches, rugged rock formations, and glorious coastal Monterey pine and cypress trees. Seeing carpets of California poppies and the fleshy leaves of ice plant ground cover, "I love it here," said Sara. "It's a sister city to Ojai." She went on about the town by the sea strewn with artists, writers, theaters and literary talent. "Good thing it's not a cloudy, cool summer day, which could bring temperatures down to the fifties."

"True. It can get cold when the fog moves in."

"Can we take a detour through?"

They stopped at a restaurant with outside seating, serving several dog owners. Ben walked Tazzie to a grassy area while Sara checked out the menu. "That's so cute that they have a food section for 'man's best friend'," she commented when he returned.

"My kinda place," Ben smiled.

They had a light lunch then took a short stroll around Carmel to stretch their legs. "Look," he motioned to a jewelry shop. "Want to go in and get you a ring?"

Her eyes followed his to the expensive window display. She looked down at her left hand, still in the sling, and laughed. "That would spruce it up, wouldn't it?"

He motioned toward the door.

"No, wait, I was just kidding."

"I wasn't. Let's do it."

"Oh Ben, I just love you so much. I don't need a ring. I have you and that's all I want. Plus, other than my watch, I never wear jewelry."

"You let me know if you change your mind and we'll go shopping." He kissed her forehead. "And about what you said..."

"Which part?"

"The 'I love you so much and all I want is you' part... Ditto, honey."

The sound of that from him was music to her ears. "So, tell me, are we going to have privacy at your brother's place."

"If you don't moan too loudly," he bantered, "we'll be okay."

CHAPTER TWENTY-SIX

Turning left on to Edgewood Drive, Ben kept his speed to 25 mph as they passed opulent residences with extravagant landscaping.

"Expensive-looking homes," Sara commented.

He slowed the engine, "Here it is," and parked in front of a stunning two-story modern ranch style with a brick-and-wood facade, opening into a small courtyard.

"Lovely." The camphor, liquid amber, and gingko trees instantly caught her attention. "It's so lush."

"Michael purchased it several years after completing his residency, when he could afford to buy here." Ben noticed a new roof and paint job. "He's just renovated it."

On the side of the property were raised garden beds with an abundance of vegetables growing. Pointing to it, "Lot of growth there," commented Sara.

"Gardening is their meditation. Stress reducer."

"Green thumbs?"

"Yes," said Ben.

Michael and his wife, Candace, also a physician, were out on the patio when they arrived.

"What's this we see?" In his late-fifties, of medium build, a man in shorts and a t-shirt opened the wrought iron gate to let them in. Patting Tazzie, "Hey there, girl, and," he held out his hand, "you must be Sara."

Sara immediately saw the similarities between them, the facial mannerisms, their angular cheekbones, and their body gestures when they spoke.

Michael moved toward his wife, an attractive woman with short blond hair and deep brown eyes, in her mid-fifties. "Candace, here's our new sister-in-law to be."

"It's so good to meet you." Candace motioned to a patio chair. "Have a seat. We were so happy to hear the news."

"Thank you," beamed Sara.

Ben smiled, "You've always told me that when it's right I'd know it. And, my sis, you were right!"

"Don't blow her ego up," Michael laughed. "You tell her she's right and she'll use it against me as leverage."

"Okay, Mike, enough," Candace smiled, accentuating her upturned nose.

Taz, discovering the bowl of water on the ground, helped herself to a long drink.

Watching Taz slurping, "Do you have a dog?" Sara glanced around for one.

"We did. He passed a few months ago. Haven't gotten rid of his things yet." Candace continued, "We left that out for yours."

"Oh, I'm so sorry to hear of such a recent loss."

"He lived to a ripe old age, our boy. It's never easy, is it?"

Breaking eye contact, Sara replied, "No, it isn't."

"What's her name?"

"Tazzie."

"She a purebred?" asked Michael.

"Yes." Tapping her knee to motion Taz back to her, Sara responded, "A rescue."

"That's all we'll have," said Candace. "Bodhi was a rescue also."

"More like a theft," Ben chimed in. "He was found tied to a tree."

In defense, Candace interrupted, "Abandoned, dehydrated and hungry."

"Okay, okay, I stand corrected," smiled Ben.

"What's Tazzie's story?" Candace asked Sara.

Appreciating how dogs create neutral ground to bring people together, Sara relaxed while she told them.

"Bodhi Gottlieb was a chocolate lab. A big fat boy," said Candace.

Sara laughed at the name, and not having referred to Ben's last name much, was curious about it. "Gottlieb, is that…"

"German," interrupted Candace. "Means the love of God, but," she laughed, "don't let that scare you. We named our dog Bodhi after a tree and not any religious figure. Anyhow, don't get me started down those tracks. It'll end in a train wreck."

"Don't get us wrong, Sara. Nothing against any specific religion, we just aren't fond of them being organized." Michael gazed at Candace. "Who was it who said they distrust people who know so well what God wants them to do because it coincides with what they want to do?"

"Susan B. Anthony." Candace wiped a fragment of leaf off her blouse. "My favorite is from Gandhi. Of course I'm paraphrasing—I like your Christ, I do not like your Christians, who are so unlike your Christ."

Sara breathed easier that this wasn't heading into a religious rant. After all she'd been through with Henry, the very mention of religion or spiritual cults got her hackles up. Although her parents were Jewish, they didn't practice the doctrine or teach her anything about it, and she grew up willy-nilly buying into whatever came along that served her at the time. This was why she gravitated to the Descartes movement, meditation, and Zen Buddhism before that—activities she involved herself in but did not adopt as her belief system. Nothing stuck, which added to her suffering when she was diagnosed with cancer—not having a ground in God or faith increased her misery. "I like that one too."

"Okay, enough religion and dog talk." Ben fidgeted with his fingernails. "It's getting late."

They all went quiet.

Michael's smile faded. "Have you phoned them?"

"No."

Michael looked askance at Sara. "Oh man." His eyes slid away from hers in an awkward silence.

Ben, responding to his brother's hesitation, "You can talk in front of her. She knows everything."

Michael remained reticent.

"Seriously," Ben urged, "I've told her."

"Edward's on a bender, the usual started Friday night."

Seeing the disgust on his brother's face, envisioning the scenario, "You spoke with him?" asked Ben.

"If you can call it that. He answered when I phoned mom. Could barely make out what he said." Michael glanced at his watch. "Ben, if he's smashed, there's no point in bringing Sara."

Hearing the repugnance in their voices, Sara was having second thoughts about talking Ben into coming.

Glad that Michael brought it up, "I think you're right, but," Ben surveyed Sara, "how do you feel about it?"

One look at the agonizing revulsion on his face was enough for her to see she'd made a mistake. *Shitty! That's how I feel.* Her body felt heavy. *What did I get him into? What was I thinking!* The last thing she wanted to inflict on Ben was more stress. *I can tell he doesn't want me to go. He doesn't want to subject me to it, but look what I've done to him!* "Do what's right for you. I'll support whatever you decide to do.

Candace interjected, "You made the trip up here for Sara to meet them."

"I'm happy we came," Sara feigned a smile. Regret moving in on her, "It's been great meeting you two." She turned back to Ben, and repeated, "I'm okay with whatever you want to do."

Candace smiled at Ben, "She's got a good attitude, this one."

"Yes, she does," said Ben. Having made his decision back at the beach, "I'll go it alone and let them know," he looked at Sara, "we're getting married."

Ben's sorrowful demeanor made Sara want to grab hold of him and tell him to forget about it. *I feel awful about this. And I feel stupid saying anything else. We're here because of me. Shit!* "I hope it works out okay."

"Me too."

Candace stood, "Come on Sara, let me show you our garden." They left the guys alone to catch up.

Michael watched the women leave. "Sara's great. I can see…"

Preoccupied, Ben interrupted, "Yeah."

Michael turned solemn. "You sure you want to go over there?"

Ben put his chin on his fist. "Oh man. I don't really know."

"You don't need to go there if it's too much for you." Ben had made it clear to Michael in the past that if he wanted to bring up his health he would, therefore Michael steered clear of asking about it. "You need to take care of you. That's what's important."

"Mike, do you think there's any chance, any possibility, that things can change? Things didn't seem to flare up when you got married."

"He was completely out of it at my wedding. You don't remember that?"

"His drunken fits are a blur."

"Why do you even want to do this?"

"Good question," Ben sat up straighter. "Being with Sara has changed my perspective on so many things. What's even possible. It's hard to imagine anything changing with Edward but..."

"I wouldn't get your hopes up."

"I won't. I just have to put it to rest one way or another." Ben had had enough of the prelim. "You did a lot of work on your place."

"Yeah," Michael told him about the renovations. "You going to take Sara to yours?"

"I didn't let Claire know I was coming," referring to a legal intern working under Ben at NASA, who he had dated a couple years earlier and remained friends with. Having the use of Ben's house was a good exchange for taking care of his mail and watering the plants.

"Does Sara know?"

"Yes, that's no secret. I told Sara that Claire is rooming with three other law students and was happy to have some space. Sara's aware we're just friends and has no issue with it."

"Maybe she'd like to see an Eichler."

"I'll ask her."

As Ben drove to his parents', the image of his drunken, stumbling incoherent father sickened him. Arriving at half-past-seven to an unlocked front door, he found his mother plopped down in a chair, outstretched skinny white legs spread apart revealing what the hiked-up skirt failed to cover, a glass of booze in one hand and a cigarette in the other, ashes falling to the wood floor. Wrinkled old newspapers and dirty laundry were littered about. The volume on the television was so loud he had to shout over it to get her attention. "Mom!"

Her glass flipped over when she put it down to grab hold of the TV remote control. "Look who's here," she slurred.

The smell of smoke, drink, and musty odor from lack of ventilation was nauseating. Cracking a window to let in fresh air, Ben uttered under his breath, "Pathetic!" He had long given up trying to do anything to ameliorate her situation, and left her to her enabling, codependent life with his father. "Where's dad?"

"I don't know," she peered through bloodshot glass eyes. No attempt was made to make conversation.

He found his father passed out cold on the couch in the den, snoring out alcohol fumes. The room was dark; the only light came from a streetlamp through a break in the drawn curtains. *Jesus, you put on a lot of weight.* Like a bum on a park bench after a night of drinking, with his huge belly hanging out over his underpants, slobbering onto himself and unaware of his surroundings—it turned Ben's stomach. Clenching his jaw, "You don't even know I'm here, do you?"

There was no response.

Ben wanted to grab and shake some sense into him, to cry out, *Wake up you slob! Look at yourself! Look what you've done to Mike and me, you loathsome wretch!* He hated the odor that lived in the walls of this house that was never a home. An inferno in his body bristled. *Get out and don't ever return. If the cancer doesn't kill you, this surely will.*

A ton of bricks pressed in on his chest as he walked the slow purposeful stride of a prisoner entering jail, to the hollow cave he grew up in, down a hallway to his old room. The door still had kick marks on it from his father's violent outbursts. Saturated in his painful past, he looked around at the dark space for what he knew was the last time. His eyes fell on a bowl he'd made in a ceramics class in high school. *I got an A+ for that, the best grade in the class.* He thought back to his dad's reaction. *You made fun of it. Said pottery was "for girls."* He felt the polished texture of the hard glazed clay, the curves he'd smoothed out, as his fingers lingered in a long goodbye. Ben made his way to the kitchen to find a pen and a pad of paper on which he left the note, "I came by to let you know I'm getting married, Ben."

Outside, he upchucked his guts on the lawn, what was left of stomach content from the meal in Carmel, and continued to retch yellow bile, sending his intestines into spasms. The wedge of his heart that his parents shattered raced hatred through his arteries, like the pain that turns a decent human being into a murderer from the furor of injustice and deprivation. Like the cancer, the insurrection in his pancreas, the stress with his father was a sickness he wanted to puke out. Grabbing hold of his abdomen to stop the cramping radiating to his backside, he left.

The minute Sara saw his defeated body language and drawn face she knew not to question him. *I see you need space.* It hurt to see him looking so caved in. *What happened?*

Candace, diverting to something insipid, picked up the slack and brought him up to date on some of their recent activities. "I'm thinking of enrolling in the master gardener program at Stanford." The mindless chatting slowly drew Ben out of his introspection.

"So, what are your wedding plans?" asked Michael.

"Something easy, probably at the courthouse."

They stayed up late continuing the simple conversation about movies, books, and Melanie, who was away at Berkeley. "Good for her for not going to Stanford," commented Ben, now feeling a little lighter.

"She broke the Gottlieb curse," Michael laughed.

The next morning, they said their goodbyes and left shortly following breakfast. Appreciating that Ben wasn't ready to talk about what happened over at his parents' house, she told him she'd like to see his home. Ben welcomed the distraction and phoned Claire to arrange it.

"Is your friend going to be there?"

"No, she's going out to grab a cup of coffee." Ben went on to explain that, "In the early fifties, Eichler homes were a branch of modern architecture. Open floor plans of glass walls."

"Was Eichler the architect?"

"No. He was a real estate developer who took modern designs from custom residences and office buildings and made them available to the general public. He used the flat and A-framed roof design attributed to Frank Lloyd Wright. Steve Jobs grew up in a home designed by Eichler's original architecture team." He continued, "I read somewhere that's one of the main things that inspired in him a passion for making beautifully crafted products for the mass market." He saw that Claire had straightened up the mess he'd left behind in his hurry to leave for Los Angeles.

"That's so interesting that Jobs' home influenced him in that way. That's some ripple effect."

"Yeah."

"What a great place. It's so neat."

Thank you, Claire!

Sara was instantly taken with the floor-to-ceiling glass windows viewing an atrium filled with colorful flowers and hummingbird feeders. "Oh look, Ben," she pointed to a green violetear hummingbird.

"That's my friend, Hector," he smiled. "I name the creatures that stop by here, a habit picked up from my niece." He watched the bird fly away. "I love Melanie, but," he continued in a melancholy murmur, "I never wanted to have children. Not after how I grew up."

Sara related to what he said, her ambivalence being rooted in her own flawed family. She was not opposed to having kids with Henry but never became pregnant while they were married, and after him, she shut down the idea of another marriage and children altogether.

They sat on a couple of old plastic patio chairs among the plants in bloom. "It's so serene here." She relaxed next to him as the stillness of the garden lifted their spirits.

His hand in hers, he whispered. "My home is with you now."

CHAPTER TWENTY-SEVEN

Driving down Highway One, what started as feeling queasy had turned into gut-gripping nausea, distracting Ben's attention from the road. When his vision grew hazy he knew they needed to stop. Having just passed the sign, Morro Bay five miles, "How 'bout lunch?"

"At Morro Bay?"

"Yes."

"The Gibraltar of the Pacific." She had walked its trails along the estuary and sunned on the unspoiled beaches years before.

Ben found a sandwich deli right on the main strip across from the quay. He went into the men's room to splash water on his face, and get his bearings from the disorienting dizziness in his head. Back outside, he saw Tazzie driven to distraction by another dog in the vicinity. Over her growling frenzy, Sara said, "Why don't you go in, get us something?"

As Ben reached for the leash his clammy hand grazed Sara's. "I'll take her back to the car."

Sara shot him a worried look. "What do you want?"

Jerking on the tether to rein in Taz, "How about we split a sandwich? You choose." Turning toward his vehicle, wet acid burned into his esophagus.

He drove out slowly across the causeway to the tied island where they parked by the big rock and found a secluded bench. Birds were nesting, gull and cormorant species, and to their amazement a peregrine falcon was pecking at debris on the ground near a trash can. "Sara, look," he whispered so as not to disturb it, "they're endangered. Most of the prohibitive avian laws are because of them." The bird stayed for a few more minutes then flew off.

"Wow, that was amazing."

Tazzie's nose went wild inhaling odors from mosses and tide pool creatures.

Referring to the familiar view of the horizon. "It's so beautiful." Sara bit into her half of the turkey sandwich.

An unpleasant fiery sensation in the back of his throat threatened retching as Ben stared down at the wrapper.

"You okay?"

Holding a napkin to his pasty face, he could no longer hide the nausea grabbing his gut. "Just a little indigestion," he mumbled.

Obvious from his wincing, it wasn't insignificant. "Talk to me. I can see you're in distress."

He though of how much he hated his parents. *What's this resentment doing to my body? My immune system?* His hands gripped the bench, squeezing it for dear life, doing to it what he wanted to do to his father. Breaking out in a cold sweat, "Oh, Sara," was all he could bring himself to say.

"I'm here." She stroked his back, trying to be comforting, but her words were wobbly. "Take a few slow breaths." He did. His pallor ebbing, a trace of pink returned to his cheeks. "That's better." She wanted him to unload what had happened at his parents'. "I'd like to hear what's going on with you," she patted his hand. "Want to tell me about it?"

Glancing around to be sure they were alone, he looked out at the ocean. "I will never see my parents again."

"Ben," she eyed his profile, "we don't know what the outcome of the study will be."

"I'm not talking about that..." he stumbled. "I don't want to ever see them again. They won't change and," he

191

choked on the words that didn't want to see daylight, "I need to let go of them." Tears came when he said, "I've spent so much of my life hating them and I see what it's done to me." Observing him struggle to get it out, Sara flinched.

Stammering, he continued to tell her what had happened at their house. "I have to stop deluding myself that there's ever going to be a satisfying resolution with them. Sara, you were the one who told me that hanging on to anger ends up hurting you. I didn't see it back then but yesterday it became clear to me. I have to wonder what's worse; how they treated me or my holding on to it, festering and poisoning my insides."

Having never faced it with such finality before brought up sorrow that made him sad to the bone, and he broke down and cried—for baby Ben who was neglected, for the little boy growing up who had no parents at his soccer games, no parents at his graduations, and no father at his birthdays. He wept for the missing parents who would never hear from him, *I have bad news—cancer*. He let out everything he had held in, and once the crying was over he felt depleted. Abhorrence, remorse, shame, and regret—the complex jumbled emotions he'd resisted his entire life— had emptied out.

"Ben, you're in a powerful place of forgiveness, doing this for your health and healing and not to get even with them. I completely understand and support you. If it came to this, then it's probably a positive thing that you went to see them."

"It was the final straw. And," he smiled at her, "you were right."

"How so?"

"It did give me closure." He thought back to their last time at the beach and what she said. *Just a visit, perhaps even closure. If you don't make the effort you may live to regret it.* "I've absolutely no regrets. I saw that I couldn't change what's happened. I can't change them but I sure as hell can change how I feel about my relationship with them. I don't want to waste any more time being angry with what I have no control over."

When another couple walked around the bend with a dog and Tazzie barked, they got going. The ride back to Ojai was quiet, with Sara musing on what had happened. Ben's reconciling and rearranging the shattered pieces of his life back into place nagged at her. The back of her head started to throb, and appearing like a dissolving watercolor painting, Jack's face dripping with sweat came to view. Screams, *Leave her alone*, melted the image until there was nothing but the sound pounding between her ears. *Stop* repeated over and over, giving her a full-blown headache. Denying a strong intuitive sense, she once again doubted herself. *My mother couldn't have known.* That part of the puzzle was still murky. *Is any of this real?* Uncertainty pervaded her.

CHAPTER TWENTY-EIGHT

The baby finally got to sleep after a long bout of fussing. Nightly, little Sara would not fall asleep. The doctor said it was colic. Her mother paced. So did her brother, waiting for the medicine to take effect, for his mother to go to sleep and for his sister to be alone so he could touch her. Never telling where his hands had been, "No one will know why she's crying."

On the occasions Rosalie walked in on him, he lied and said he was trying to help his baby sister relax, that he heard her whining. Those were the nights he was frustrated, because he didn't get to finish. When the intruder didn't interrupt him, he touched the baby and became aroused. He liked playing with himself until his thing got hard. Once excited, he'd leave and finish in his own bed. Night after night, he'd return...

Startled, Sara was relieved to wake. *It happened! I know it happened! These are real memories surfacing. Holy shit!* At just after three in the morning, with Ben asleep beside her, she reflected back on the nightmares. *The surgery must have triggered them.* The loss of her breasts— her sensuality—latched onto the intrusion of her body during infancy. Sara had not been able before to make the connection to her promiscuity, her need for sex to feel loved, and the sexual molestation. Without each piece of the puzzle in place, the process of unearthing her denial was slow in coming. Hammering away at the repressed trauma in sleeping trances, unraveling the psychic pain, had taken over two years.

At first the dreams made absolutely no sense to her. As they progressed, however, the revelations became clearer, repeating until she accepted what had happened, and that her mother knew. At long last there would be no more denying her sixth sense. The time had arrived for Rosalie to be called to account.

The day moved on with Sara traipsing back and forth, anxiety building over confronting her mother. She removed the bandage and prodded her ribs, grateful that they were healing nicely. It was the fortitude she needed to help her deal with the asphyxiating angst. A couple more days and she could keep it off. Reaching to put the dressing back on, Taz grabbed hold of an end. "Stop that!" Sara yelled. "Let go!" She went off at the dog in a loud and frantic tirade, sending Tazzie crouching out of Sara's bedroom.

Ben stuck his head in the doorway. "You okay?" Sara had told him everything, solidifying the actuality she was really going to do it, stand up against her mother.

"Yes," she paced.

Furrowing his brow, he gave her a look.

"No! I'm not okay!"

"Want a foot rub?"

"I don't think I could lie still for it."

"Anything I can do?" He moved closer.

"Not really. I just need to do it."

"Want me to stay with you?"

You've been subjected to enough, Ben. "Nah, I'm okay, but I think Tazzie could use a friend."

Looking down the hallway, out of Sara's line of vision, "Taz is on her back, belly up, fast asleep." Turning to leave, "I think I'll join her."

The escalating nervous energy intensified after Sara phoned her mother and said, "I need to talk to you."

"So talk."

"I want to come over and do it in person."

"Ben coming? How is he?"

Oh that's just great. You want to know how Ben is and not me! Furious and approaching a meltdown, she felt her legs quavering. *Breathe. Get a grip.* She took in a slow, long breath, held and released it, *Let go of the anger.* "He's okay." Another deep inhalation to calm herself barely impacted. "I'll see you later."

Watching the street signs as they approached her parents' house, "I don't know how I'm going to keep it together."

"You'll do fine. I have every confidence in you."

"Thanks, Ben."

"I'll be close by, at the park around the corner. Phone me when it's over."

Arriving to the coffee wafting through their home, Danish pastry on the table with three places set, her father out at the racetrack with friends, the first thing Rosalie said, "Where's Ben?" pissed Sara off.

You don't ask a thing about me? Not one "how are you!" Sara fought the urge to pick up one of those fancy antique vases and shatter it across the wall. Restraining herself and in a very controlled way, "Let's go sit," she headed to the living room, away from the food.

"You don't want coffee? A bite to eat?" superficially droned her mother. "Ben on his way in?"

Breathe. Stay calm. Sara turned, "Ben's not coming in."

Sara knew what she wanted to say, the script rehearsed in her head over and over. Her well-chosen words were no match for the recoil from the betrayal and abandonment, the unrelenting loss she grew up with.

Trapped for years, worried how the fallout of a confrontation with her mother would affect her father, she knew she needed to face it, step into courage—for once, put herself first. Knowing it was not going to be easy, she relied on the hope that things would work out for the best, and she'd live with the results come hell or high water.

Stay calm. "Mom, you know that I need to work on stress reduction if I want to get well." Sara was not just referring to a remission or cure from the breast cancer, but also an inner health. Just as Ben had come to terms with his family situation, the work Sara needed to do now was forgiveness. Without putting to rest the fundamental question concerning why her mother stood back all those years, there could be no forward progress.

Rosalie said nothing, her attention wandering around the room.

"Mom! I'm talking to you. Can you at least focus on me while I'm speaking?" Sara waited for her mother to face her. "There's something we've never discussed that I'm going to bring up and I need you to hear me. Please…"

"Say what you have to say!"

Sara finally lost it. *Oh I'll say it all right, you fucking bitch!* "It'd be nice if you would park the attitude!"

"You came here to talk?" Rosalie's eyes turned into a pointed Uzi ready to fire. "So talk!"

The volcano had been building: the bad dreams, the sleepless nights, and piecing it all together. The lid shot off the pressure cooker and out it violently gushed. "Why did you let Jack molest me!"

Rosalie's body jolted back, her mouth flew open, and she made a move to get up and leave.

Sara stood to stop her. "Oh that's great, just walk out! Walk out on your daughter with cancer!" Sara's parched voice cracked out, "Where's your compassion!"

Pivoting around with a vengeance, "My compassion?" Rosalie laughed a psychotic squeal. "I protected you!"

Sara, seeing the torment in her mother, stumbled in disbelief. "Protected?"

Rosalie turned ashen. She made a fist and pounded air in an attempt to release the words stuck in her throat. Grabbing hold of her top and pulling it away from her chest, nearly ripping it off, she fell to her knees, breaking out in a wail to wake the dead.

Sara teetered over to her mother. "Tell me."

Rosalie bawled, "I protected you." Spasms of grief, rivers of tears from years of silence ran wildly out of control.

"How?"

"We had him committed," Rosalie howled. "I committed my own son!" She collapsed into a torrent of weeping.

Sara sat on the tile floor at her mother's side and waited for the storm to pass.

When Rosalie was composed enough to speak, "I knew all along what was happening. It would have killed your father. The doctor said he couldn't take another heart attack. I tried to keep Jack away from you." Chin bent into her chest, "I placed monitors in both your rooms, hidden from where Jack would find them, but they failed to alert me when I dozed off. I couldn't stay awake twenty-four hours a day!" Refusing eye contact, Rosalie went silent, shaking her head, trying to cast off the heinous memory.

Seeing Rosalie's squinting gesture, Sara whispered, "What?"

"I fell asleep," she cried, "while he did that to you, his own sister!" She went on about how Jack continued the abuse when the voices in his head took over. "I heard him talking to himself and knew what I had to do. God help me." She told Sara that she went to see a doctor to set a plan in motion. Once that was done, she let Irving know that Jack was schizophrenic and needed to be committed. She had sedative pills ready to give to her husband to ease his reaction. Irving lived through Jack's institutionalization but Rosalie was never the same. She blamed herself for giving birth to a girl that her son molested, for having to put him away, and for not knowing how or doing better by both of them. After that she became closed and bitter.

"Does dad know about what he did to me?"

"No."

Sara recognized that what she and her mother had in common was protecting Irving, and now she also understood why he drowned himself in work. *He needed to get away from the house, from mom. Not from me.* Sara felt compassion replace resentment with the understanding of the hell her mother had lived through. When she tried to put an arm around Rosalie, her mother resisted, but this time Sara didn't take it personally. She knew her mom had to resolve her own issues and it would take time. Sara pulled back, "Thank you."

What seemed like a lifetime of more crying passed before Rosalie faced her daughter with a pained look that spoke, *I'm sorry.* For Sara, it was liberating to see. Hearing what Rosalie finally got off her chest and understanding her father's absence all those years was redemption.

When Ben arrived he found Sara and her father having tea at the dining room table, chatting and smiling. Rosalie was in the bedroom resting.

CHAPTER TWENTY-NINE

Sara relaxed on the drive back to Ben's hotel room and filled him in on what occurred with her mother. "I think they put new bulbs in those streetlights," she laughed. "They're so bright."

Seeing out of the corner of his eye that she was giddy with relief, "You're what's lit up."

"It turned out better than expected. I feel like I've lost a thousand pounds. She's never opened up to me like that before."

"She needed to," he slowed into the parking area of his hotel.

"She's still stuck, Ben." Sara noticed the lot was almost full. "What's going on here?"

"There's… a medical… convention over at UCLA," he gasped.

"What's the matter?"

Ben pushed against the seat to relieve the pressure in his back radiating from his belly. "Just a stitch," he evaded the question, "nothing to worry about."

Sara mistakenly assumed it was from the negativity they'd both been involved in the last few days, "Okay, no more talking about family."

"That's a deal." He got out, stumbled, and reached for the side of his car to steady himself, before moving to open her door. The rest of the way to his room was uneventful.

Sara fell asleep the minute her body hit the bed until Ben's tossing and turning woke her in the middle of the night. "You're soaking wet. Let's get you out of those pajamas." Putting the back of her hand to his forehead, "You're burning up."

Ben moaned and writhed, unable to lessen the intense discomfort under his right rib cage.

Sara rushed to the bathroom and came back holding a glass of water and aspirins, a washcloth draped over her wrist. "Take these." Wiping the cloth over his body to cool and help him get comfortable was of no avail. He could barely tolerate the touch on his skin; the pain was too searing. Frantic, she went for the dry weed and bong.

Ben's plaintive expression stopped her. "It has a quick onset," she stuffed and lit the water pipe and handed it over to him. "Take a long drag off this."

He did. And another. In close to thirty minutes he told her he felt moderately better. Relieved his fever had cooled, she felt calmer. She covered him back up and sat with him until he fell asleep. Several hours later, Ben awoke to people talking outside his room. It was a little before eight, Thursday, and Sara had a treatment at UCLA in the afternoon that he refused to have her cancel.

Worried that he looked so sapped, "Ben, you should be seen right away," Sara pleaded.

"No, I don't want you to miss your appointment. We'll go when you're finished. I just need to rest. A lot's been going on."

"That's true." She thought of the Palo Alto trip and the scene with her mother. Not wanting to entertain otherwise, denial once again protected her from intuition hollering that it was more than the emotional sewage they'd just dealt with. "You're probably right. Let's get you some room service and take it easy till I'm done."

They arrived at Zimmerman's office at half-past-five and the nurse ushered them in. Zimmerman took one look at

Ben, the tinged jaundiced skin and his sunken eyes. "You were doing okay a couple days ago?" he asked them both.

Sara nodded affirmation. "Up in Morro Bay, he had an upset stomach from stress." She looked to Ben to see if she had misread him. "Ben?"

Ben knew he needed to be honest with his doctor and Sara. He could no longer insulate her from the truth by hiding what was happening in his body; the distress was too great to keep pretending and covering up. "It started up in Palo Alto." He gave Zimmerman a day-by-day account, that by the time they were in Morro Bay he had no appetite—even with pot the nausea was hard to control, and had progressed into abdominal pain. He eyed Sara, who recounted what had occurred the night before.

The curtain had risen and in plain view the stage was set for her to see what was going on. No longer could she buy into the story that family strain on both sides was the probable cause. *Oh God, please.* It was hard for her to accept and as much as she wanted to turn away, stay hidden in her rationalization that stress was aggravating his health, perhaps just causing a temporary setback that he could get beyond with his treatments, she now knew better. Putting on her medical hat scared the hell out of her.

Zimmerman's eyes held compassion as he rested a hand on Sara's shoulder. Then focusing on Ben became his primary objective. "Okay, let's have a look. Take off your shirt." He had him lie down on the exam table to palpate his abdomen. The percussion over his liver produced a dull thud, which told him there was more solid mass in there than just liver tissue. When he turned him on his side to tap on his back, Ben flinched and drew his knees up to his chest. "That hurt?"

"Yes."

Zimmerman had to assist Ben to sit up. "I'm ordering some labs and a scan of your abdomen. You can go to St. John's and get it done." He turned to Sara. "Do you think you can handle our patient for a little while?"

Sara nodded and grabbed Ben's arm.

"I've got a few patients to see over there. I'll check in with you when I'm finished. Wait for me in radiology."

At St. John's, Ben had blood drawn, and in agonizing discomfort stripped down to slide into the cylinder tube that scrutinized and imaged his body. Forty-five minutes later they were in the radiologist's office with Zimmerman.

Hunched over, hugging his gut, Ben asked, "So what's the verdict?"

"Your blood work shows you're anemic."

"What's his red blood cell count?" Sara asked, knowing that several things contributed to anemia in cancer patients—the cancer itself, the treatment, internal bleeding, the body making fewer cells, and a combination of any of these. She also knew this changed with remissions and was not, in and of itself, a gauge of prognosis but more a general picture of the current state of the patient. When Zimmerman said 3.2, her stomach turned over. *He'll need a transfusion.*

"The scan?" asked Ben.

It was obvious from the tight-lipped expression on his face that this was the part of Michael Zimmerman's job he hated the most. "Ben," he hesitated, "I'm not going to mince words."

"It's okay, just say it."

"There are several new masses on your liver. But that's not what concerns me."

Feeling like her chest caved in, Sara strained her neck muscles to move enough oxygen in to help her focus. The tone in Zimmerman's voice, the way his words moved out slowly, told her more was coming and it was not going to be good.

"That back pain you felt during the exam is another mass around your celiac plexus."

Ben looked confused.

"It's a bundle of nerves grouped around the aorta where it passes through the opening in your diaphragm. The problem with this is pressure from the mass can build up and cut off circulation or make breathing difficult."

Not anticipating this degree of sudden bad news, Sara became lightheaded. Grabbing hold of the chair to steady herself, she realized that none of her experience had prepared her for this.

"What do you suggest?" asked Ben, who barely comprehended the overwhelming information. He could not make sense out of the fact that death was knocking, and was not retreating with the research study or injections.

"You need to be admitted to get a transfusion. Let me run some follow-up tests and we'll give you something to help with the pain."

"What are we talking about here?" He coughed up the next words, "I mean, how long do I have?"

Trying to deflect the conversation, "Let's just get you settled in and comfortable and talk about this later."

Ben would have none of it and unprepared for what would come, he asserted, "I want to know."

With both of them staring at him, Zimmerman reluctantly drawled, "It's hard to know for sure." He crossed his arms over his chest in a protective gesture used by doctors when they're withholding bad news. "This is like Russian roulette."

"Meaning what?" asked Ben.

Zimmerman's pupils dilated. "It could be a month, maybe two, probably not more."

Ben turned white.

Unable to gather her wits, Sara asked, "You're sure there's nothing else we can do? What about other studies?" Zimmerman shook his head.

"What do I need to watch for?" With attention on Ben, her heart cracked into millions of tiny particles scattering incomprehensible thoughts, blinding her from fully grasping what was occurring.

"For now, let's just get him admitted and comfortable. Take it one step at a time and hope for the best."

The best? What could that possibly mean? Sara, no longer containing her tears, *How could this be? How could I have missed this? It can't be!*

Zimmerman looked at Sara, still in her bandage. "I think you're safe to remove that and drive if you need to. Just take it easy."

The room went silent as Zimmerman wrote out the admission orders. All that was happening was a blur to Ben, as the reality started to set in. Sara took hold of the paperwork. "I'm going to stay with Ben tonight. Can you please see if you can get him a private room?"

With sagging shoulders as though the weight of a boulder was on him, Zimmerman connected with her devastated eyes. "I'll do what I can."

Ben was admitted to a single bed room. When he was settled in, against Sara's resistance and urging that he just relax, he insisted she get him a pen and paper. Numbed by shock, and against her better judgment, she yielded to get it over with so he would calm down.

On it he wrote a handwritten will. Ben knew exactly what he needed to do to make it valid. He wrote while he was hooked up to a transfusion, and Sara went outside to phone Ellen to fill her in on what was happening and see how Tazzie was.

On hearing Sara wanted her to call Rosalie, Ellen asked, "You sure you don't want to tell her yourself?"

"I need to get back to Ben. Just tell her I checked in with you because of Tazzie."

Sara returned to the room to be directed to get two witnesses for what he had written. With two of the floor nurses present, Ben read to them out loud before he had them read separately and sign, "I, Ben Gottlieb, being of sound mind and under no undue pressure, hereby declare this is my will. I give to my mother, Bertha Gottlieb, the sum of $100. I give to my father, Edward Gottlieb, the sum of $100. I give to my brother, Michael Gottlieb, the sum of $100. The balance of my estate I give to Sara Phillips." Ben then signed and dated it in front of the two witnesses. He had them do the same and indicate they saw him sign the will in their presence. When they left the room, "I'm giving that amount to my parents so they can't contest it, saying they were overlooked. Mike's fine with me doing what I want to. He doesn't need the money."

"I don't either. You don't need to do this. Please don't feel obligated. All I want from you is for you to just quiet down and get your strength back."

"I want to do this," he insisted.

"Shh now, okay, please calm down."

Reaching a weak hand to her cheek, "And if I make it out of here, I still want to marry you."

Sara was perplexed that he still wanted to get married when he had just taken care of his original reason for it—to have his life's work mean something after he was gone.

"That's enough for now, Ben."

Seeing she was puzzled, he refused to concede until he had his say. He wanted her to understand. "I want to arrange for you to also receive my NASA retirement and life insurance. Once we're married, I'll sign the paperwork to make it happen."

"Ben," she repeated, "I don't need you to do this."

"I want to. I worked hard for what I have. I want you to have it. I know you'll put it to good use."

"Okay, please simmer down now."

"One more thing."

Looking at his deep blue eyes, luring her to him, tugging on her heartstrings, she desperately wanted him to relax, to try to get better, so they could have another day together. "No more, enough already."

"This is the last thing."

"You promise?"

"Yes. Please phone my brother. Tell him he doesn't need to come down. Tell him I love him, Candace, and Melanie. And that I have you here and that's all I need."

"Okay, Ben, now please rest."

CHAPTER THIRTY

The night moved into morning, bringing with it the clanking noises from breakfast carts and trays. Nurses and doctors made their rounds tending to patients while the loud speaker failed to muffle its roar, waking everyone not drugged enough to sleep through it. The cacophony of hospital life, upsetting to most patients, was a rhapsody to Ben's ears. Cuddled in the single bed next to Sara, he awoke with rosy cheeks, doing better from the morphine coursing through his veins and happy to see the sunshine. "It's a good day to be alive."

She kissed him full on the lips. "Every day with you is just that."

"You look tired. The ribs hurting?" he asked, as it was her first night without the bandage.

"No, actually I'm fine in that department. As long as I don't exert too much."

Just then Zimmerman walked in appearing bright-eyed. "The transfusion did the trick. Your red blood cells are back in a low normal range."

Ben remembered the needle prick in his vein earlier that morning. "I thought I was dreaming a bee stung me," he smiled. "So, Doc, do I get to go home?"

Aware that Ben was staying at a hotel in Westwood near UCLA and that Sara lived an hour away from there, mentioning hospice was not what Zimmerman wanted to suggest, it was too early. "Where's that going to be, Ben?"

"At my house," interjected Sara.

Not having thought through how he wanted to handle it and concerned over Sara taking it on, Ben didn't want to burden her. "Wait a minute."

Shaking her head, indicating that any other suggestions were closed topics, Zimmerman responded, "Okay then, let's get those discharge papers signed. Schedule a follow-up appointment with me Monday at my office. And I'll be sending you home with some medications to help you feel better."

"For pain?" asked Ben.

"Yes." Zimmerman went to the door and turned around. "I'll also give you something for the nausea."

His grave face, showing he wished he could do more, needed no further words.

Looking at Zimmerman's troubled countenance, Ben's voice cracked, "Thank you."

"Okay, my honey, let's stop the butt flashing and get you out of that gown." Sara pulled out her phone to let Ellen know Ben was being released, and to have her get in touch with Rosalie. "Phone me back after you speak with her." Sara's phone buzzed twenty minutes later. "What took you so long?"

"Your mother." Ellen slurped from the cup of coffee she had made for herself.

"Oh man, now what!"

"I told her I just heard from you."

Sara listened to Ellen describe Rosalie's diatribe.

"I told her you wanted me to ask her to stop by Ben's hotel room and bring his clothes to your place."

"And?" asked Sara.

"She kept asking me, 'What's with all this phoning from you and not my daughter?' and when I said you were busy with Ben, she argued that you phoned me. I told her it was 'cause I needed to ready the house for him."

"Ay, I hate to put you through this but I'm just way too tired to deal with her."

"You shouldn't have to, so don't worry about it."

"Did she say she'd do it?"

"It went downhill when she asked who was going to pay the bill and I suggested she put it on her credit card. She grumbled something then hung up. I'll phone the hotel to verify it's been done."

"Thanks, El."

"Anytime. Anything. Even your asshole mother," Ellen laughed.

Rosalie and Irving arrived an hour after Ben and Sara to find Ben on the couch in the living room with Tazzie up next to him. Relaxed from the morphine and transfusion, Ben watched them put his things in the entrance hall.

"You don't look too bad, Ben," was all Rosalie said, her head rotating in search of where her daughter was.

Smiling at them, "Thank you for doing that," Ben motioned to stand.

"Don't get up," Irving stepped into the living room, "we were glad to help you, son." He peered back at Rosalie who made no move. "She's distracted," he smiled to Ben.

Seeing the strain on Rosalie's face, Ben told her, "Sara's in the kitchen making lunch."

"Thanks," Rosalie responded and went to find her.

Irving sat facing Ben. "I'm sorry you're not feeling better. So is Rosalie but she doesn't deal very well with these kind of things. Better she's in the kitchen with the women for now."

The way Irving made eye contact, expressing softness, was a gentle reassurance there would be no drama between mother and daughter today. "Thank you, I understand."

Irving nodded, his body language communicating that the understanding was mutual. "If you want for anything, if there's anything we can do for you, I see how happy you've made my little girl," reaching out a hand to Ben's shoulder, "you let us know."

Never having had a father figure connect with him before, this with Irving was extremely soothing to Ben. "I can't tell you how much that means to me, Mr. Phillips."

"Irving. Call me Irving. So now, please let me know if there's anything."

Ben didn't want to be an imposition and tried to tell him as much. "Irving, I wouldn't feel right..."

Irving flipped a hand up in the air, indicating enough, and smiled when he said, "Don't listen to Sara or my wife about what I can or can't do. I'm no invalid," he laughed. "I think women need to invent problems so they have things to deal with. I wouldn't offer if I didn't want to help." He pushed back in the chair to make himself more comfortable. "Is there something, Ben?"

"Thank you, Irving. There is something." He went on to say he'd written a will in the hospital and given it to Sara. Explaining that he wanted everything he has to go to her, he told Irving that his friend Carl up in the Bay Area would be the attorney to contact when the time came. "We went to Stanford Law School together. He's one of the best there is."

"What do you want me to do?"

"I want you to make sure Sara gets the will to Carl. She was hesitant, maybe because I didn't leave much to my parents, but trust me, they don't need it. I don't want my life's savings to go to waste. I know she'll do good things with it and make it mean something."

"Okay son, we'll take care of it. And if there's anything else, just name it."

Ben, circumspect by nature, was wary to overly tax Irving with anything else.

Irving instantly responded to Ben becoming quiet. "I see a familiar pull-back in your demeanor, son. I know it well. It's the same way Sara and Rosalie act when they don't want to stress me, which ends up creating more stress than if they just treated me normally and capable of functioning in the first place." He met Ben's silence with another smile. "I guess this is where I need to reassure you. I'm really okay to help you. Trust me when I say I want to, I mean it. Doesn't do me any good to sit around at home like a lump on a log wasting away. I need to be productive like everyone else. Helping you, helping my girl, Ben, there's nothing more important. Please do let me know if there's anything else. We all want you to feel better."

Ben wiped away the streams of gratitude running down his face. "I don't know what to say."

"No need to say anything if you don't want to but if there's something you want me to do, I'm here."

They sat together quietly, while Ben let the rivers of emotions wash over him. "Thank you." Having felt Irving's genuine acknowledgment, Ben knew he was authentically understood and it was okay to continue, "If you're sure, there is one more thing."

Irving nodded.

"I want to marry your daughter."

Irving, taken aback for a moment, "This is what you want to do? Shouldn't you just concentrate on resting up?"

"You sound like your daughter," Ben laughed. "I want to do this so my retirement plan goes to her. I've explained it to Sara."

"If you're sure…"

"I am. I really am. And I could use a hand in arranging it."

They talked about what was needed to get the application for the marriage license and a date set at the Ventura County Clerk's office.

"You have your paperwork here, Ben?"

"All that's required is a valid government-issued picture identification. We can use our driver's licenses." Ben looked at Irving and hesitated.

"Is there something else?"

"It needs to be arranged as soon as possible," he paused, "but if this is too much for you…"

Attempting to mask the sadness on his face, Irving glanced down at his pant leg, pretending to wipe away a piece of lint. "We'll handle it." Returning his gaze to Ben's, "This will give Rosalie something to do. Keep her out of trouble. I have a request in return for you."

Ben could not imagine what that might be but knew if it were anything he was capable of, he would move heaven and earth for the person who'd be there to help Sara when she needed it. "What would that be?"

"Call me dad." Irving reached an arm out across the space that separated their seats and gave Ben a fatherly pat on the shoulder.

Overcome with appreciation, too choked up to speak, Ben nodded consent.

Clearly comfortable in his skin, Irving chatted about insignificant things to occupy the time. "I see you've made friends with Sara's dog."

Petting Taz, who remained beside Ben, "Yes, they've both adopted me."

"Sara's a good girl. She's had some rough times. But things seem to be turning around." From the kitchen, Rosalie's loud talking distracted him. "Sara mentioned she'd had quite a conversation with her mother the other day." Irving looked through the wide arched entrance leading to where the women were. "I think they both needed it. Things haven't always been easy with our son."

Seeing that Irving seemed okay to broach the subject, Ben followed suit. "I understand you haven't heard from him for a while. I hope that's good news."

"I think it is, Ben. He seems to be taking his medication regularly now." Irving took in the aroma of something cooking, "That smells delicious. What are the girls making?"

"I'm sure it's something healthy." Satisfied after having this chat with Irving, Ben understood with a greater depth why he'd fallen in love with Sara. She had her father's heart.

They heard the women talking over each other. The salmon was grilling in the oven and Ellen mashed the Yukon Gold potatoes, while Sara cut the broccoli to steam. Rosalie got off the stool she was sitting on at the counter to stand over Ellen. "Why'd you get those? They're harder to mash."

Coming to the rescue, "No they're not, Mom."

Taking a potshot, "Well, I always use russets," Rosalie went for a spoon.

Ellen, adding more soy milk to smooth the consistency, whispered to herself, "Does everything have to be such a damn dramatic production with you!"

Rosalie scooped a mound of spuds, "Needs more salt." She glared at Ellen, "I thought you took cooking classes."

Curtailing her mother's attitude, "That's enough, Mom," Sara looked askance at Rosalie.

Vocal cords visually vibrating in her neck, Rosalie screeched, "It needs more salt!"

Ellen, tightening her grip on the utensil she was holding, gave Sara a look.

"No Mom, Dad can't have that much." Sara knew that her mother was not going to change, that she was a control freak and had to have things her own way, but the wounds inside of her spiritual bosom had eased since their confrontation. The barbs unwittingly thrown by her mother no longer latched on. *I hope to God that you find your own inner peace, Mom.*

Ellen put on a CD of Yo-Yo Ma playing *Bach's Cello Suite No. 1 – Prelude,* which thankfully set the pace for the rest of the evening.

CHAPTER THIRTY-ONE

On Monday morning, after Ben's appointment with Zimmerman, the County Clerk's Office received a phone call from a well-connected, influential government official to expedite the license and date for a wedding. "Make it happen this Wednesday." The man who phoned was married to one of Zimmerman's patients. Everything set in motion made for smooth sailing when Irving contacted them.

With the help of his medication, Ben was able to sleep, keep food down, and have pain-free days. Missing initially, as he regained strength sexual intimacy crept back into their relationship.

Still panting, he said, "I'm glad that the drugs aren't wiping out my libido."

"Ben, it's a good sign that you're even up for this."

"Ha ha, that's a first-class pun."

"No seriously. Sex drive is healthy." Her lips moved over his flesh. "You felt okay, I mean, for real?"

"Sexually? Yes. I'm aware of the effect of the chemicals in my body. It feels different, perhaps a little muted, slower in coming. I'm pleasantly surprised. I didn't expect..." The glow still radiating between them, he expressed, "It's a testament to how much I love you, Sara."

"You know, Ben, maybe you're going into remission. Perhaps all that stress did predispose you to a bad spell and well... Zimmerman could have been off. Maybe what he saw wasn't on the money? Who knows?"

"Hold that thought," he whispered. "Is it uncommon, what's happening?"

Sara thought back to the cases she'd dealt with and decided that the only path worth taking was the high road, entertaining the positive. Not being able to answer him with any certainty as an indication of what was possible, the only thing that really mattered was how well she was doing, and with that she said, "I know that after I started the study and was feeling better, I woke up one night aroused and masturbated. It was also slow going at first and I got uptight that I might have lost my sex drive. I refused to give up, refused to sink into the mental shit that told me I'm doomed."

"I gather it was a success?"

"Yes," she laughed, "but honestly that's when I sensed I was going to be okay. We can have days where we're better and other days not so good. Illness doesn't have to define either of us." She ran a hand over his chest, the soft curly hair between his nipples, and she tingled where she had just exploded. "I do know that sexual activity is an indicator of health. There's a lot of data to validate this, research and anecdotal studies."

"I like that." He took hold of her hand and pressed it against his lips. "I like that a lot."

"I'd say, all things considered, you're doing great."

"You're being out of that bandage isn't hurting anything either," he laughed.

Kissing his chin, moving down, relieved he wasn't in pain and was tolerating their intimacy, "I told you you'd get lucky."

"Ahh," he nestled her head in his hands, "that feels so good."

Day by day, Sara's passion grew, and so did her effort to please him. Pushing aside thoughts that robbed them of quality time, they discovered new ways to be tender and trusting. Lying beside him, she purred, "We're creating great memories."

"Yes, we are," he kissed her forehead. "I hear crickets. Let's go see."

"Have you ever seen a cricket?" she laughed.

"Yes, I have, even in daytime trying to hide in the grass."

Out on her deck, she said, "Ben."

Watching the sky streak pink and fade to gray, "Yes."

"I just wanted to say your name."

"Be my guest, honey."

As the last of daylight moved below the horizon, the night's din grew louder. "You like the sound of insects chirping. I like the sound of your name."

Wrapping an arm around her, "Do you know why crickets chirp?"

Pressing his hand, "No, but I'm sure you're going to tell me."

"Contrary to popular belief, it's not from rubbing their legs together. It's the male calling to the female."

"You're having me on."

"No seriously, the male's wing is constructed with ribs and scrappers that make the noise. They even have different tones, the loud song to attract the girl, soft courting when she's near, an aggressive chirp to ward off other males, and a different one after they've copulated."

Looking up to his watchful, inquisitive face scouting her lawn for the source of what his ears were hearing, "You're not messing around, are you?"

"It's fascinating when their symphony grows louder, one of the many voices of the night. I wondered about it and looked them up on the web. The more I study things in nature, I see how alike we are, especially the noise they make after the sex part," he chortled.

"My own private all-living-things tutorial."

"Yeah," he breathed in the scent of orange blossoms.

"We're so lucky we both love the outdoors."

Spending as much time outside as they could brought them to a synchronicity with every living thing. Ben motioned to the cypress tree off the deck, "We give it carbon dioxide and it gives us oxygen."

"I know." She felt her chest's motion. "The dance of life. So beautiful, Ben."

In accepting their fate, and directing their attention to the real world as it moved moment to moment, they found inner peace, with each other and individually.

Wednesday came with Sara dressed in beige linen slacks and a light pink silk blouse, Ben in his khaki pants with an azure polo sport shirt, highlighting his blue eyes.

"We're ready," yelled Sara, and when Ellen trundled down the hall with Tazzie in tow, she was surprised. "Look at my girl! So cute!" On the sly, Ellen had made a pink dog top for Taz, on which was an inscribed heart, *Congratulations mommy Sara and daddy Ben.*

"Aww, Tazzie, you look spiffy all decked out." Ben turned to Sara. "And you," he gave her the once over, "are gorgeous as ever."

Piling into the car, Ellen drove, with Ben, Sara and Tazzie in the back seat. "It's great that they're letting you bring Taz," said Ellen as they made their way to the County Clerk's Office.

Rosalie and Irving were waiting in the corridor outside the room Ben and Sara were to be married in. They were overdressed for the weather, she in a knit suit and he in wool pants and a shirt with a tie. Sara was sure that was her mother's doing. On seeing Sara approach, Rosalie reached out and touched her daughter's pants. "Linen, for once you're dressing nicely. You should do this more often."

Irving grabbed Rosalie's arm and moved her through the door.

"Give me the word and I'll muzzle her," Ellen said, tightening the rein on Taz. "Or better yet, throw her down the stairs."

"Shh," Sara laughed it off.

Inside, Ben paid the forty-five dollars for the short and sweet ceremony, followed by hoorays from the staff as he kissed his bride.

Back at Sara's for a celebration around the dining room table, Ellen poured everybody sparkling apple cider. "A toast," she raised her glass. "To my best friend, Sara, and her hubby, Ben. May love stay with you always, no matter where life takes you."

"Here, here," added Irving.

"I'll drink to that," Ben laughed. "But let me add," he looked at Sara, "to my wife, the woman who brought meaning to my life and taught me that time isn't measured by the clock but by the moments of shared love. I love you, Sara."

Seeing Rosalie dab her eyes with a napkin, Sara was overcome with emotions. "I don't have adequate words…"

"Saying nothing works for us," smiled Ellen.

The evening moved on with carefree chatting until Sara saw her father yawn. "It's late, how about spending the night?"

"We don't have pajamas or a change of clothes," protested Rosalie.

"I've got things you can wear," and when Sara saw her mother in one of her t-shirts and baggy sweat pants, she cracked up.

"You'll asphyxiate in that." Irving continued joking, "She won't sleep naked," throwing them into hysterics.

Ellen offered up, "You want to try something of mine?"

"You're larger than Sara," Rosalie gave her a stern look.

"Oh come on Rosalie," Irving pinched his wife's rear, "let's have a look at you in something I can easily get off."

Rosalie, whacking his hand away, broke into rare laughter. It didn't last. Seconds later, in her usual form, she stretched out the pant leg a good eight inches from the side of her body and sarcastically asked Sara, "When are you going to get rid of these junky clothes?"

"Go to sleep, mom."

The following morning, they had a light breakfast before Irving and Rosalie left and Ellen drove Sara to UCLA for her treatment. Ben phoned his brother and Candace to bring them up to date. There was no mention of his parents.

Arriving home to find a couple of electrical cords leading out to the back deck where Ben was blowing up an air mattress, Sara asked, "What's this?"

Scrunched down by the inflatable bed, he looked up at her. "Our honeymoon. I've been busy planning the perfect trip."

Ellen came out to see what was going on. "What's with the floor heater?" referring to the one he had next to where he was working.

"Don't trip on that," he pointed to the electric wire leading to the plug in the house. "It's for later when it gets cooler. I don't want my bride to freeze."

"You're too much," said Ellen. "Come on Tazzie, let's go for a walk."

With the sun slowly setting and the moon rising, Sara felt the air start to chill. "You're sure it won't be too cold for you out here?"

"We'll be okay." Turning on the heater for show, "See, it works. Just in case."

Knowing how much he loved nature, how it lifted his spirits, she wanted to accommodate him, to help him be a part of it as long as she could. She bent down to kiss him and turned the heater off. "Probably won't need this."

"We'll keep each other warm counting stars till we drift off like birds perched for the night."

"Nicely said, my poet laureate."

"You just gave me an idea." He finished with the bed, plugged the nozzle, and rose to leave.

She watched him take his time to get up, using his hand to steady himself holding onto a deck chair. She was glad they weren't dwelling on how he was feeling, hour-to-hour; he didn't want to. He made that very clear when he told her it didn't help him. He didn't want to regurgitate what had already happened and focusing on where he was heading was counterproductive. Since the medication was keeping him comfortable and his mood was good, that worked for her. "Where you going?"

"You'll see. It's a surprise."

The nearly full moon cast enough light for Ben to see the piece of paper in his hand. As they lay snuggled into a down sleeping bag atop the airbed, "Here's my other wedding present to you." He then recited:

In the shadow of eve you found me
To the light of morn you pulled me
From the bare cave of my loneliness
To the fullness of your meadow we fled
    To romp in the grass
    To smell the flowers
    To fly like birds
    To count the stars

"What a beautiful surprise. You wrote that today?"

"Yes." Looking to the starry night, "You see there, it's Orion. I gift it to you, a forever keepsake. Whenever you want me," he pointed up, "I'll be there."

She kissed his cheek, shoulder, arm, everywhere her lips could go over his jaundiced body. "Including every last star, that's how many lifetimes we'll have together."

"That's a great big universe out there."

"Exactly," she cuddled into him.

"Do you know that our Milky Way galaxy has around two hundred billion stars in it? Not to mention other galaxies, astronomers estimate that there are approximately one hundred billion to one trillion."

"Okay, Mr. NASA, you made your point."

223

"Nope, I made your point. I just quantified forever," he laughed.

They talked and listened to the sounds of the night and awoke to the sun beating down on them. Tazzie now by their side, the coffee permeating from the kitchen, "God bless, Ellen," said Ben.

"Yes, she's a wonderful friend." The fullness in Sara's heart was inexplicable. *Were it not for Ellen, none of this with Ben would have happened.*

The three of them sat outside and had their coffee with toast. "My brother's coming down," said Ben. "I told him not to but he insisted."

Sara knew Ben had spoken with Michael when Ellen took her to UCLA. "What about his schedule?"

"He cleared it. Candace is coming with him."

"When?" asked Ellen.

Sara, grateful for the lull in the storm, watched Ben contemplating what he was about to say, looking better than when he arrived back from the hospital. She appreciated how none of this, our existence, is under our control. One minute you can be dying and the next a miracle happens in the form of a remission, a new drug, or some other stroke of luck. She also knew that Ben's good attitude helped his immune system function to better hold at bay what would otherwise ferociously march in.

"They should be on their way," he responded.

They figured out the arrangements for all of them to be at Sara's. Ellen would continue to work the next two days, sleep over, and spend time with them on her days off. When Ellen tried to insist that she could go back to her place, "You're family, El," said Sara, who would not have it any other way.

CHAPTER THIRTY-TWO

The coastal fog bank was late in clearing, leaving behind a sultry, midafternoon air, thick with humidity and enervating Sara, in the kitchen prepping salad for dinner. Ben was resting outside and Tazzie hadn't left the front door since Ellen went to work. Her barking alerted Sara that Michael and Candace had arrived. Entering, they were instantly impressed by the arts and crafts appearance of her place. "Very nice," said Candace. "Hey there," she bent to pet the dog, "little miss rottie."

"It's hot here," commented Michael, leaning in to hug Sara.

Sara felt the moistness on her body, running rivers of perspiration. "More humid than usual."

Michael wore a worried, squinting expression as he looked around for his brother. "Where's Ben?"

He was on the wooden swing at the back of the lawn.

"You didn't see him when you pulled in?" Wiping her hands on the apron she was wearing, Sara took it off and threw it over the nearest chair. "Come on, let's go find him."

The grass, soggy from watering, sloshed under their feet as they made their way to Ben. "You have a creek," Candace eyed the grounds, "and so many trees. What a great piece of property."

"You can hear the water flowing when it rains, which isn't that often."

"Yeah, the drought's a problem down here," commented Michael, noticing the dry patch by the rose bushes.

Catching sight of Ben a few feet away, slouched over with his eyes closed, Sara raised her voice, "Wake up, sleepyhead." His non-responsiveness panicked her and in a knee-jerk reaction, she rushed to him. "Ben!"

Michael spun around from looking at the flowers, and ran full force to his brother. Nudging a shoulder, he instinctively felt for a pulse. "Ben," he shook him harder.

Lethargic and jaundiced, Ben slowly stirred. "Oh wow," he slurred. "Hey, Mike, you're here." He looked at their frightened faces. "I must... have fallen asleep."

Sara was still shaking from the adrenaline rush. "You okay?"

"It's hot out," Ben pulled his wet t-shirt away from his skin. "I don't do well in this dampness."

"Where's your water?"

Ben barely moved his lips into a sheepish grin. "I left it..."

Michael put an arm around his brother. "Let's get you into the house and get some fluids in you."

Sara's attempt to assist Michael was circumvented by Candace stepping in. "Why don't we let Michael help Ben?" Once they were out of earshot, "I wanted to talk to you."

"The weather isn't helping Ben." Sara's legs grew weak. "He's also off chemo now." *It's got to be the heat. He seemed okay when we made love last night.*

"Yes, Ben told us that was his decision on the phone."

"He doesn't want any more needles or hospital visits."

"That's understandable," Candace shifted her position out of the sun's glare. "How are you doing with this?"

"Me?" Sara wiped sweat from her face, "I'm okay." She didn't want to dredge up the reminder she lived with daily that Ben's time was running out. "I think we're both doing okay, considering."

"Let's sit down here," Candace motioned over to the swing. "I'm concerned about you."

The weight of a sumo wrestler pressed in on Sara's chest. "Please don't be... We're managing." She rested in the hope that a miracle could happen. *There could be another study, a spontaneous remission.* She didn't want to entertain any other thoughts, even though her head told her differently and inside, in her gut, she knew what no one needed to tell her. Her heart and head disagreeing with each other raged a war.

Seeing the torment in Sara's eyes, "If you need to talk..." Candace's tone emphasized urgency. "The stress could interfere with your own health. I'm not just here for Ben," she asserted, "I'm here for you as well. We caregivers need support also. Please let me help."

Knowing Candace meant well didn't change the fact that Sara felt cornered. Although reluctant, she knew she needed to communicate to put Candace's mind at ease. She opted to open up about her own situation. "I need to be able to trust you."

Softening her demeanor, "You can," responded Candace.

"I think I'm going into remission so please don't worry about me."

"That's great, Sara."

"Last week the scan showed regression of several hot spots. Of course, I'll need follow-up scans but I want you to know I'm okay. I can handle what's going on with..." Teary-eyed, "I love him so much."

"Oh Sara, sweetie. It's very difficult. But I'm relieved to hear about your news. Ben must be happy about it."

228

"I haven't told him."

Surprised, Candace flushed, "Really?"

"No, I don't want to put the focus on me. I don't want to jump the gun and then be disappointed if it's a fluke. I won't do that to him. I just found out last week. We're managing and not talking about our illness with each other. I told you so you wouldn't be troubled about how I'm doing."

Candace pulled back, "Don't you think he'd want to know?"

"No! Please, Ben doesn't want to talk about being ill. He never brings it up. What's the point? We talk about other things." She tried to clear away the lead balloon stuck in her throat. "We don't need to bring up the obvious. I start to talk about my news and he withdraws." Wiping tears, "And it's not yet definitive with mine. If that happens, I'll inform him. "

"I appreciate where you're coming from. I won't mention anything though it's a good idea to share it with him when the occasion is right." Candace reached over to put a hand on Sara's. "How about we take a little walk around the property to give your bloodshot eyes a chance to clear up?"

Michael, in the bedroom with Ben, watched him nod off.

"Did you talk… to Zimmerman like," Ben sucked saliva from the side of his mouth, "I asked you to?"

Michael tried to veer off the topic. "How 'bout getting some rest and we can talk about it later?"

"What'd he… say to you?'

"I don't think this is a good time to…"

"I want to know."

"Ben..." Michael stopped himself.

Adjusting a pillow, Ben sat up straight, determined to stay awake, "Mike, tell me."

A reluctant, solemn reply came from Michael, "Two weeks."

Startled, convinced he had longer, a little more time than that with Sara, "You sure?"

Michael, clearly upset and not wanting to continue, "That's what Zimmerman said."

"You wouldn't have told me?"

"No."

"I don't understand." Ben glanced out through the pulled venetian blinds. "We've been having sex. I thought that was a gauge."

"Maybe Zimmerman's off."

Ben became aware of the lavender growing near the street and Michael's voice faded. Swarming worker bees drank nectar, and Ben thought *those bees are going to be around longer than me.* Trembling from the rush coursing through his body, "How long you planning on staying?"

"As long as you need us. We're both covered."

"Did you tell our parents how I'm doing?"

"No."

"They got the note I got married?" The mere idea of Sara, the vision of her face, calmed him.

"Yes," Michael broke eye contact.

"I take it, it wasn't pleasant."

"Ben," Michael's attitude pleaded, "let it go. The last thing you need is a stressful discussion about what ranks top of our tension Richter scale."

"He was drunk when he read it? Tell me, Mike."

"You are tenacious. Good old Edward," Michael emitted sarcasm, "was smashed and disgusting. He had nothing intelligible to say. Okay?"

Ben reached out a droopy hand to Michael's thigh and gave it a pat. "Thanks, I needed the reassurance I was right."

"Well you were right."

"Mike?"

"Yes."

"I'm fine with it," Ben smiled. "I mean that."

"I'm glad to hear it," Michael nodded. "Now how about you get some rest?"

"Okay."

"And," motioning to a filled glass on the nightstand, "keep drinking that water." Michael found the thermostat was eighty-eight degrees in the house. *No wonder you feel like crap.* Turning on the air conditioning, he set it for seventy-two.

The women arrived back to a comfortable temperature and Ben back up at the couch, doing better. "I told you I didn't do well in this hot weather."

The rest of the evening involved a light meal, conversation, and soft music. Around nine, Michael said, "I think it's time to hit the bed."

Ben and Sara were out on the deck, with Michael and Candace in Sara's bedroom when Ellen got off duty and quietly made her way to the guestroom, ushering Tazzie in with her.

Ben was wide-awake.

"Aren't you tired?"

"Yes, but I'm not ready to sleep." He stroked the velvet texture of her cheeks, her slightly upturned nose, and outlined her full lips. Too sluggish to do anything else, he sighed into her ear, "You're the best thing that ever happened to me."

"Ditto, my hubby," she looked up at the starlit night.

"Even though I'm hubby number two," he murmured.

"Oh Ben, I was so young then. What I had with him was nothing compared to the depth and completeness I have with you. I never felt joyful with him like I do with you." Turning to make eye contact, "With you I'm certain I'm meant to be exactly where I want to be. That's never happened before. I'm a different person now than I was then. You helped me find myself and work through so much. It's difficult to explain."

"I'd say you're doing a great job of it."

Looking at the orb of night reflected in his pupils, "I've often heard the expression 'the light within' but never fully understood it. Not till being with you," she stroked his arm. "Now I see that my happiness rests inside me, in my heart, and it's not from someone or something external. Your support brought me to the core of all I'd been escaping from my entire life, things too painful to deal with. Until I saw and went through that, I was nothing but a shell. Henry and the men before you were chemical cocktails superficially filling my emptiness. With him I was always slightly off kilter and uncomfortable. It took my being with you to see that. And yes, I was wounded and raw in the end, when he left me, but those wounds were already there. He just poured salt on them." She kissed Ben's cheek. "That's history now, thanks to you."

Seeing tears moving down her face, "I didn't want to upset you."

"Upset?" she laughed. "I've never been happier."

"Aww, honey." He caressed her face with his hands and kissed her. It was a deep and loving kiss, filling her with the energy to last a lifetime. No wounds or scars impeded his forever love from entering her. "It needs no further explanation. I feel it also."

Feeling his body against hers, their legs touching, "Why'd you bring that up now?"

"I think it's the only thing we haven't talked about. I wanted to be sure you didn't need to communicate with me or might be avoiding it because of how I'm doing." He kissed her forehead, ran his mouth down the side of her face to her neck, where he lingered. "What you've just said is a valuable gift for both of us."

Sara nestled her head next to his. "This gesture from you, this very simple beautiful act of caring kindness and loving support is one of a zillion reasons why I adore you."

"Oh good." With effort, growing weary, he joked, "How about enumerating the rest of them."

"For starters," she raised his hand to her lips and kissed it over and over, displaying the overwhelming affection she felt for this wonderful man. "And there's more where that came from."

A peace moved over him, an inexplicable energy, a sixth sense, without fear. "Did you ever wonder if there's life after death?"

Transcended in this union with Ben, she spoke from a place where mystery is revealed to those who see with open hearts. "I've had patients on their deathbeds, moments from the end, who woke up, literally sat up, and told of conversations they just had with their loved ones who had already passed away. They wake from comatose states with a lucidity that boggles the mind. It does make you wonder."

"I feel something, Sara." He inhaled her skin, fresh and inviting. "There's a knowing, something I've never experienced before, a certainty that we'll never be apart." He looked at the moon, glowing down on them, a couple of days from its fullness. "I don't understand why I'm so tranquil inside."

As if God tapped her on the shoulder, she recalled and told Ben about a story she had read of a five-year-old boy who had remembered a past life vividly. "There was no way anyone could have fed him that info. No one in his family or close circle of friends had any knowledge about the things he mentioned from another country. He described a house with detail that an investigative reporter validated. The clincher was the memory came to him in a different language." Awe-inspired, she rhetorically asked, "What's that about?"

The clarity he lacked moments before came into focus when the miracle of life and mystery of death fused and he realized that this eternal now is forever, without separation. He saw that which is not available to the human senses— waves of light, decibels of sound, the structure of an electron—the space between heartbeats where eternity lives were present yet not perceived, not with a body and its restraints. Illumination, beyond time and matter, the force that flows through bodies but is not defined with limitations had ignited him. He knew that his feelings for Sara had brought him to this place, where the physical dies but the bond continues.

With his breath caressing her neck, she noticed a movement in the sky. "Did you see that?" She lifted a finger to direct his attention to a shooting star.

"It means we're soul mates, destined to be together for eternity."

"That's right. The heavens know what's true."

That night stars danced and melded into billions of pulsating living organisms, friends beckoning them. What they saw was endless, timeless, mysterious life—and it was filled with love.

EPILOGUE

Zimmerman's prognosis was off, and Ben went on to live another seven weeks. Michael and Candace visited until they saw he was stable and Ben insisted, "Go on home. I'm okay."

During that time Ben experienced laughter, nature watching, meaningful conversations, and lived to hear Sara tell him, "I'm in remission." The news from her scan came two days before he died peacefully in her arms, surrounded by his new family—Rosalie, Irving, Ellen and Tazzie. His last words to Sara were, "See you later, my love."

Nightly, as the stars grow bright in the darkened sky and Sara relaxes into sleep, she gazes out of her bedroom window to watch Orion twinkle. It is then she is reminded of the first time she met him, the handsome stranger in Zimmerman's waiting room, when she glanced over to the form he was filling out to see *his name was Ben.*

POSTSCRIPT

In 1998 a drug without disabling side effects was approved by the FDA for treatment of advanced metastatic breast cancer in women with a certain protein that causes the cancer cells to grow very fast. Some of the subjects in the trials experienced a slowed progression of disease while in others the cancer completely disappeared.

About the Author

Paulette Mahurin lives with her husband Terry and three dogs, Max, Bella, and Lady Luck in Ventura County, California. She grew up in West Los Angeles and attended UCLA, where she received a Master's Degree in Science.

While in college, she won awards and was published for her short-story writing. One of these stories, *Something Wonderful,* was based on the couple presented in *His Name Was Ben,* which she expanded into this fictionalized novel in 2014.

Semi-retired, she continues to work part-time as a Nurse Practitioner in Ventura County. When she's not writing, she does pro-bono consultation work with women with cancer, works in the Westminister Free Clinic as a volunteer provider, volunteers as a mediator in the Ventura County Courthouse for small claims cases, and involves herself, along with her husband, in dog rescue.

Profits from her books go to help rescue dogs.

Made in the USA
Lexington, KY
17 August 2017